CHARLEY'S CHRISTMAS WOLF

A Macconwood Pack Novel

C.D. GORRI

xoxo,
C.D. Gorri

Charley's Christmas Wolf

A Macconwood Pack Novel #1

by C.D. Gorri
The Macconwood Pack Novel Series
Copyright 2015, 2021 C.D. Gorri, NJ

Dedication

To Valerie Finn, thank you for entering my title contest.

Before you start reading, don't forget to sign up for my newsletter!
www.cdgorri.com/newsletter

Blurb

Rafe Maccon is the Alpha of the Macconwood Pack, *for now*. **His rule is being questioned by a rogue Wolf who wants him ousted for breaking an ancient law that states the Alpha must be mated!**

He must find a mate in order to keep his position. Seeing their Alpha in trouble, Rafe's Wolf Guard take it upon themselves to find one for him.

Charley Palmieri works a dead-end job and lives alone with her cat until one night when her world is changed forever.

Instant attraction sparks between them. Can Rafe convince Charley to be his before the meeting of Pack elders on Christmas Eve? Will she be his one true mate, for life?

St. Lucia's Day – December 12th

He circled the woods once more. His black coat gleamed in the silver moonlight as powerful legs carried him quickly through the frozen terrain. The battle was finished. Another few months of peace and prosperity won together with his allies. All it cost was the blood and sweat of his Pack.

He thought of the young Wolf who had asked for his help. She was tenacious and brave. This was the first time in a hundred years such alliances had been made. He knew he had made the right decision for his Pack. The only way to go into the future was to move forward.

Wasn't that what his father had always said? He tasted blood on the air and tensed. Some of it he recognized. It belonged to his Wolves. But they were whole. That was all that mattered.

The black Wolf reached out with his mind and felt his Packmates' injuries. *No casualties*. The blood-stained ice that covered the forest floor and the sulfuric stink of dark magic invaded his nostrils.

He snarled and quickened his pace. For a moment or two the Dark Witches had almost had them. But they had triumphed. The others were gone. Only his Pack remained. They waited for him. Their *Alpha*.

He slowed down as he entered the wooded enclosure. Pride vibrated in his very being. These Wolves were brave, fierce, and loyal.

As his Guard moved to flank him, Rafe Maccon threw back his head and loosed an ear-piercing howl. It spoke of loss, of triumph, of the end of an era and the start of a new one. This had been his last battle as a warrior.

The time had come for him to fully assume his rightful position as Pack Alpha. His father's death years ago should have triggered that leap in his status, but he had denied his birthright for as long as he could. He had chosen to fight with his Wolves instead. But the time had come for him to lead them.

According to the local White Witches of the Coven Realta, the prophecy had already begun. He and his Wolves needed to ready themselves for whatever came next. He signaled to his Beta and like always, he immediately understood what was needed of him.

Rafe watched him leave with a few select Wolves then he surveyed his Packmates. They stood in front of him, each one muscular and strong with varying shades of fur ranging from palest white, tawnies, reds, and browns to his own midnight black coat. One by one, they lowered themselves on their haunches, lupine heads bowed. He had earned their respect before, but tonight he had gained their undying trust. Now, he had to keep it.

Chapter One

Thunder clapped overhead. A mix of hail and rain began to pour from the quickly darkening skies. The streetlights flickered and the tiny overhead shelter at the bus stop gave no protection whatsoever from Mother Nature's latest onslaught.

"Not now! Come on!" Charley cried.

She huddled into the thick pink cardigan she wore over her one good dress. It was a wool blend which was bound to get ruined in this weather. She had instantly fallen in love with the way it alternately hugged and flowed around her curvaceous body. She especially loved the scalloped hemline.

It reminded her of classic movie stars like Hepburn and Taylor. She used to watch them all the time with her grandfather. She smiled as she looked down at the outfit. The pale ivory suited her dark eyes and hair. The weather was definitely going to ruin it. And on her meager salary it would be months before she could replace it.

She looked down at her matching heels and stomped her foot as puddles began to form on the uneven concrete sidewalk. *Great! That's just perfect!* It just wasn't her day, or her year for that matter.

It was almost Christmas and the nutty weather still hadn't made up its mind what season it was. One day it was in the 90s and the next the thermometer had dropped to the low 30s. The past few months had been very unusual for the typically predictable New Jersey climate. Charley didn't know what to make of it.

She was sure it was because of the holes in the Ozone or global warming, melting snowcaps, and the cattle crisis. Every newsfeed had someone to blame, but not much was being done about finding a solution. She shook her head, thoughts like that were better off left to scientists and people who could actually make a difference.

Charley was just trying to make it through a date. Well, a *blind date* that she didn't even want to go on. And she was already late for it because her boss at Junior's Famous Italian Deli, the third "Junior" as it were, just had to make her clean all the slicing machines and the display cases twice that day!

Not to mention he had her mop the entire floor, flip the chairs, hose down all the rubber mats, secure the freezers and refrigerators, and lastly, Windex the tall storefront windows inside and out! *Ugh*. Only then did he let her leave. And the rat hadn't even paid her.

The deli would be closed for the next six weeks. Junior and his family would be in Italy to oversee maintenance work on his family's villa. *Wasn't that nice for him?* Charley had to bite her tongue all day from telling her boss what she really thought of her forced, not to mention unpaid, vacation.

She barely had enough time to get to her apartment, shower, and change before the bus was scheduled to arrive. Dinner had better be worth it!

A black van pulled over across the street and idled. *Lucky bastard!* Charley sighed as she gave it a brief look. The van had tinted windows and chrome finishes. From where she stood, the engine purred.

Not the usual racket from the delivery vans she dealt with at the deli. *Too nice for this neighborhood,* she thought. *Heat probably works too.*

She tried not to stare at the driver. From what she could see, he was huge and rough looking. And boy, was he looking at her. *Pervert! Yeah, have a good look, buddy!* She thought as she tugged her sweater closer to her body.

She tried in vain to cover her ample assets. No doubt they were clearly revealed through her soaked dress. The bus stop provided very little protection indeed. She turned her head towards the street, as if just looking could somehow make her bus appear. No such luck.

The van remained across the street unmoving, creepy driver and all. Charley shuddered. There was no traffic, foot or car, on the usually crowded Jersey City intersection. It was cold, wet, and dark and she was all alone.

She dug in her purse for her cell phone just as lightning lit up the sky. It was followed by the booming sound of thunder and Charley practically jumped out of her shoes.

The distraction was enough that she didn't see the van pop a u-ey and pull to a stop right alongside her. She didn't hear the door open or see the man with the blonde spiked hair exit the vehicle.

He moved faster than any man should be able to and grabbed her from behind. Charley's heart pounded as a huge hand clamped down tightly over her mouth. She struggled and tried to scream. Cold fear ran down her spine as he dragged her to the now open side door.

"Sorry about this," a deep voice said, and he scooped her up and sat down with her on his lap. She tried squirming, but arms like iron held her still.

"Why this one? I thought the blonde was better?" said a rough voice to her right. She struggled to turn her head but got nowhere.

"No way, dude, he doesn't even like blondes. Not since Stephie. You remember her, that blonde viper was a backstabbing little bit-," said another male voice coming from the front seat.

"Shut up guys! Okay hon, I'm going to take my hand off your mouth and we're going to ask some questions, alright? Nod if you understand."

Charley nodded. She was scared out of her mind, but she wouldn't go down quietly. She waited for him to release her. As soon as he lifted his hand, she opened her mouth and screamed as loud as she could. She threw her head back directly into the nose of her captor.

"Shit! I'm bleeding! Hold her, dammit! No, don't hurt her, get the rag! The rag! Shit!"

Charley dove for the door handle, but the stupid thing was locked. She fumbled for a second, but it was too late. Large hands grabbed her and before she knew it, she was in a grip even stronger than before. Angry tears streamed down her face.

"Let go of me, you perverts! Let me go!!"

She continued to try and twist out of her captor's grasp, just then one of them held a rag over her nose and mouth. Then it was *goodbye, Charley*. Literally.

Sometime later.

"Dude, look!"

"Get ready."

"Hey, she's coming around."

The sound of deep voices pounded inside of her aching head. Charley struggled to open her eyes. *What happened? Where am I?* Her thoughts were all jumbled and confused. She felt awful, like she did after taking a nap when she had a really bad headache.

Charley sprang up from her prone position. That was a mistake. She grabbed her head. It felt like it was going to explode.

She looked down at her lap and saw she was wrapped up in a way too big, green flannel robe. And, yup, except for her panties, she was naked underneath.

"Oh, shit. Here she goes," a resigned voice said.

Charley opened her eyes and took in the mountain sized men surrounding her. A split second passed before she opened her mouth and screamed.

"Aghhh! Who the hell are you people? Oh my God, I've been kidnapped!"

"Now, now, take it easy," one of them stepped

closer and Charley screamed again and flung a pillow at him.

"Back up, buddy! Okay, six huge men, well that one looks like a baby," Charley spoke to herself, but the one she called a baby stiffened.

"Hey, I'm twenty!"

"Wait! Seven! There's seven of you? *1, 2, 3, 4 ,5, 6 and 7!* Okay, don't move," Charley closed her eyes, her mind trying frantically to figure out what the heck was going on.

Seven men had abducted her and brought her to a house. A nice house actually. She opened her eyes again and from her place on a rather huge bed she looked at her surroundings.

A soft down-comforter and pillows in various shades of blue covered the bed, navy and beige curtains hung from large windows, the floors were natural stone, and a huge fireplace crackled cheerfully in the corner. Not so bad, considering she was a prisoner!

"What are you going to do with me? Why am I here? Where are my clothes? Why did you—"

"Wait, let me explain—"

"Oh my God, you're going to kill me, aren't you?!," Charley looked around, but the only thing she could get her hands on were more pillows. Not really helpful when trying to fight off giant kidnappers.

"We're not going to hurt you, okay. None of us are even gonna touch you," said blonde-spike guy.

He had two wads of cotton stuffed up his bloody nose. *Aha, the grabber!* Charley focused on him. Oddly, there was no bruising on his face or around his cotton stuffed nose. And she was sure she had broken it.

"You think I'm going to trust you? You sick pervert! If you're not gonna kill me what are you going to do, huh, rape me? Keep me chained up? Cut me up? Cook me?"

"Jesus, lady, what do you think we are? Animals?" laughter followed.

Charley turned her head. She squinted her eyes as she recognized the six-foot plus man with long, brown hair and his equally long beard.

"Wait a second, I know you! You come in every Thursday for the roast beef and fresh mozzarella!"

"Heck yeah! Best sandwich in a hundred miles," he nodded and grabbed a turkey leg off a plate. He shoved the entire leg in his mouth and pull out the bone clean. *At least he chewed with his mouth closed.*

"Alright, if you're not going to hurt me, then just let me go. I swear I won't tell anybody about this stupid little prank. I promise," Charley knew it wasn't likely, but hey, worth a try.

"Look, we're sorry about all this, but we need you," the youngest of the bunch spoke.

"For what?" her voice came out low and squeaky, but she didn't flinch.

"For our Alpha."

"What are you guys, like, dogs or something?"

"No. We're Wolves," Spikey smiled at her, bloody cotton and all. She wondered if his gleaming teeth didn't grow a bit.

"Uh huh. Okay, I need to be going now."

"You can't go," beard boy spoke up. He seemed sad, but serious all the same.

"Why not? Look, you guys are crazy. I need to leave. I really need to leave, please."

"Just imagine for a second that you believe us, okay? We really *are* Werewolves, and our *Alpha* is about to be usurped by this real assho- not nice guy. You see, according to our laws an Alpha can only rule absolutely when he is mated. Understand? He *needs* a mate in order to take his legitimate place as Alpha and *you're* it. Surprise!"

Charley stood up. Seven pairs of eyes watched her. There was beard guy; spikey bloody nose boy; the teenager; a glowering male who was thinner than the rest and meaner looking; the one talking now who had short sandy blonde hair; and two giants who sported identical killer grins and shocking red hair. And they all believed they were Werewolves. *Oh crap.*

"You're all crazy!"

C.D. GORRI

A growl sounded to the right and she noticed the twins' lips pulled back in identical snarls. Charley clasped her robe tighter and backed up a step.

The slam of a door startled the entire group. All the men stood up a little straighter except for sandy. He stood and rubbed his face.

"Damn, he's back early," he said quietly.

The knob turned and a man entered the room. The breath rushed right out of Charley as she took him in with her eyes. There stood the biggest, most gorgeous man she had ever seen.

He had dark hair that skimmed his jawline. Chiseled features enhanced by five o'clock shadow, and eyes that made her knees wobble. They were deep set and icy blue. She swallowed and looked down. Afraid she'd get lost in those eyes.

Next came his shoulders. They were bigger than any professional football player's, hell, maybe even *two* football players'. Charley had to bite her lip to stop herself from sighing out loud. He was a perfect male specimen. Like something out of a Greek mythological hero story. *Hercules or Odysseus.*

Even then. Charley was sure they had nothing on the man who just walked into the room. He stopped dead in his tracks when he saw her. He shook his head and rolled his eyes. *Okay, not very flattering.*

"Oh shit, you didn't," he grabbed sandy by the

collar, lifting him an inch off the floor and he growled. Yes, *growled*. 'Sandy' dropped his eyes to the floor and bared his throat, hands held up high as if in surrender.

"Damn it, Seff! You kidnapped another one?" his voice seemed to shake the entire room. That was all Charley heard before she hit the stone floor.

Chapter Two

Charley rubbed her eyes. The back of her head ached as if she'd hit it. *What a crazy dream!* That's what she gets for agreeing to a blind date. She must have been stood up or something.

How *did* she get home? She stretched. *Mmm, so warm.* She always wanted a real down comforter. Especially this winter when temperatures dropped to single digits almost every night. *Wait a minute, when did she buy this anyway?* It was always one of those things on her wish list, but she could never really justify the expense.

She opened her eyes and looked around. Panic gripped her as ferocious blue eyes as light as a glacier reflecting the sky stared at her. Those glorious eyes were set in the perfectly sculpted face of a man bigger than anyone she had ever seen. Charley inhaled.

"Aghh-," a hand the size of a baby watermelon clamped gently over her mouth.

"I'm sorry, but please, no more screaming. I have a terrible headache," his voice was deep and sincere, and he seemed exhausted. She almost sympathized with him. Till she remembered she'd been kidnapped.

She nodded as much as she could. His hand smelled good. A woodsy, clean scent filled her nostrils. Like cut grass, and Christmas trees, and fresh split wood rolled into one. *Whatever. Focus girl!*

He removed his mammoth hand and Charley looked him over. He sat perched on a wooden chest next to the bed. The seven not dwarves were nowhere to be seen. She was alone. With *him*. She pulled the sides of the flannel robe tighter.

"Oh, well gee, I'm sorry. Seriously, excuse me, *you* have a headache! Allow me to be a little more cooperative with you. After all I *asked* to be kidnapped, dragged into a van, rendered unconscious, stripped of my clothes and held against my will!" by the time she was finished Charley was yelling, out of breath, and ready to hit someone.

A small smile played at the corner of her captor's lips after her tirade, but it quickly turned into a frown. She liked seeing that small smile and the knowledge she had been responsible for it warmed her insides. His glower, on the other hand, did not.

"*Who* stripped off your clothes?" he growled in a deep baritone.

She was embarrassed to admit it was not all that unpleasant a timbre. Especially if under the right circumstances. *Stop it, Charley.*

"I don't know! What part of *rendered unconscious* did you not understand? And—"

"I'll be right back," he was up and walking out the door before she could finish.

Chapter Three

Charley was alone. She should have been scared, but what she felt was something more like annoyance. And she was thirsty. Small wonder after all that screaming.

There was a large glass of water on the side table. She downed it in three gulps, reveling in the way the icy smooth liquid soothed her raw throat. She wouldn't have minded something a bit stronger considering her circumstances.

She took a good look around. The bedroom was large, more like a suite. The décor was masculine, expensive and sturdy too. *Not bad, but no liquor cabinet.* Not that she was much into the stuff anyway.

The fire was lower now than when she first came to. She looked down at the green robe she wore. Her dress and things were nowhere in sight. Then it hit her.

She was *alone*! She needed to find a phone! She looked on both end tables, inside the drawers and closets, but there was nothing. No landline, cell, tablet, or computer of any kind.

She did find an antique clock on the fireplace mantle. It was beautifully carved with a scene that was like something out of a fairytale. She was getting quite a lot of that! Anyway, it showed huge Wolves in mid-run through a dense forest. One massive wolf was in the lead, his head thrown back in a fierce howl. She ran her fingers delicately over the wood. *Beautiful.*

Charley's hands trembled as she traced the carving. *Werewolves.* She shook her head. *Look at the clock's face, look anywhere else, Charley. Do not get caught up in this mass delusion!*

Ten-thirty. She had made it to the bus stop by six. Over four hours had passed since then. That mattered very little in the greater scheme of things. No one would be looking for her with Junior's closed.

She lived alone except for Buttercup. That old cat wouldn't notice until his food bowl ran empty. She grimaced. The door opened and tall, dark and crazy came back in.

"I thought you'd like to know that Cat, my little

sister, was the one who undressed you. Your clothes were wet. They worried you'd catch cold," he had the decency to look abashed.

"You do realize that the police won't care that my kidnappers were considerate, right? It's only a matter of time before they come looking for me," Charley bit her lip, but her eyes never wavered.

Hey, some people would consider a deli counter girl an important person, right? After all, she did cut the thinnest, most perfect slice of prosciutto in the whole state of New Jersey!

"You know, it's funny you should say that Carlotta. And, whereas, I am greatly pleased by a well-made sandwich, I somehow don't think you'll be missed, at least not for a while. Junior's will be closed for what, six weeks?"

Charley gulped and closed her eyes. *Dammit. Now what?*

"So, what, Mr. Kidnapper? People will miss me."

"Rafe. My name is Rafe and let's face it, Carlotta, no one is waiting for you," she heard the sympathy in his voice and Charley stiffened.

"How the hell would you know? And where am I?"

How dare he talk to her like that! He didn't know her! He didn't know anything about her! He was nuts, gorgeous, but nuts!

"We're at Maccon Manor, my home. It's in South Jersey. The town is called Maccon, named after my ancestors. We're on the outskirts."

"How original."

"It's my main headquarters, but all the Were-wolves under my care, are welcome. The Macconwood Pack consists of all the Wolves on the east coast of North America. There are about 500 of us in town. The total population is about a quarter of a million. I govern them all. I am their Alpha," his eyes glowed and Charley gasped.

"Great, the *Jersey Shore*, not just a reality TV hell hole, but a haven for Werewolves and their boss who happens to kidnap strangers for shits and giggles!"

His laugh resounded in the room. A deep and pleasant rumble. He walked closer to her. His huge shoulders took up so much space, Charley backed up without meaning to.

"Oh, Carlotta, we are going to get along just fine. But I am sorry you were brought here against your will. You deserve much better."

"Great. You seem decent, you know for a kidnap-per, so how about you let me go and I'll send you a Christmas card or something?"

He shook his head and crossed his arms, looking her over from head to toe. Pride held her still despite the need to squirm. She brushed her hair back behind her ears and wished she had looked in a mirror before he returned. *Seriously? Get a grip, girl!*

She was desperate enough to accept a blind date just before Christmas, but Charley was not delusional. Well, not enough to believe she had been kidnapped and brought to the Jersey Shore by a Pack of Werewolves. *Not yet anyway.*

"I promise I will do everything in my power to see that you are protected and treated with care. My Wolves were only doing what they thought was best. I'm sorry. I'm out of time."

"Oh, okay, they were only doing what was best. Excuse me, where are my manners? How dare I express outrage at being kidnapped! So, what now? You bite me and I'm a Werewolf too? We go howl at the moon and chase rabbits?" she tried and failed to not sound hysterical.

"Actually, I love chasing rabbits, but you can't be *made* into a Werewolf. You have to be born one."

"Awe, gee, well, this was fun, but since I'm not a Werewolf, and neither are you really by the way, then we just can't be *mated*. So sorry, but I'll just go now. I was kidding about the police. Really, nobody needs to know."

"Actually, human females are very desirous to Werewolves. Humans are better at producing live young. Female Werewolves have a difficult time with pregnancy. A sad, but accurate fact for my kind. As Alpha, I must have a mate who can give me an heir."

"I'm sorry, what? Do you really think I am going to stay here? So, I can give you *live young*?"

"I'm afraid you have no choice. The simple fact is, I need you."

Chapter Four

"*Riiight*. So, if you're a Werewolf prove it."

"Excuse me?"

Hands on her hips she glared at him. She could forgive the whole chauvinistic rant about a female's purpose being to produce live young. After all her own grandfather had told her time and time again that she needed to get married and have babies. But there was no way she was giving in to the whole Werewolf thing. *So, yeah, let's see you get down on all fours buddy!* Damn if that didn't turn her knees to jelly too.

"Prove it. Now."

"I can only change during the full moon."

"Really, isn't that a little cliché?"

"Rumors sometimes hide truth, Carlotta, and the moon will be full very soon. Believe me I *know*. Her phases are ingrained on my very soul, *mmm*," his head hovered over Charley's bare throat and he inhaled deeply.

"You smell like heaven."

Heat kindled in her belly and worked its way up through her entire body. He inhaled again and moaned like she was a fresh batch of cookies. Charley backed up another step. It was not a good move.

The back of her legs hit the bed and she sat down abruptly. The folds of her borrowed robe flew open and revealed long, shapely legs. He reached forward and took her hands, effectively stopping her from rearranging the fickle fabric. He was so warm! She glanced up. His eyes. They were *glowing*!

Charley sucked in a breath. Was it too early for Stockholm syndrome? Because right now all she wanted was for him to close the distance between them and *well*- she didn't know what exactly, but yes, she wanted it alright. He inhaled again.

"I know you find me desirable, Carlotta."

"Conceited much?" she tried to shake it off, pretend it wasn't there. But it was no good. He seemed to know what she was thinking.

"It's not conceit. I can smell it. *Mmm*. No, don't move," his voice was a low dark bass that throbbed up her spinal column.

"Why not?" she crossed and uncrossed her ankles, her nervousness growing with each step he took.

"Your scent. Every time you move, I get more of it. Oh God, um listen. Carlotta—"

"No one calls me Carlotta," she spoke softly, completely enthralled by his face.

He squeezed his eyes shut and kept his head back as if he were trying to create space between them. A losing battle as his body leaned towards her. *Another deep breath.*

"Everyone calls me Charley," she hated the way her voice shook, but she couldn't deny the tiny tremors of excitement that vibrated all over her body.

"Really? That's a shame. Carlotta is a beautiful name. It suits you," he moved closer. It was as if he was being pulled by some invisible force. He opened his eyes. They seemed to glow a shade darker than their usual icy blue. Maybe it was a trick of the light?

Charley licked her parted lips. She leaned back further onto the massive bed. It was as if she had no control, her body was reacting to his in a way that was new to her. And she liked it. Her elbows dug deep into the plush mattress as Rafe's massive body loomed over hers.

"I am sorry, Carlotta, that I can't give you more time. I *must* be mated before the meeting on Christmas Eve. I'll give you anything, everything you've ever wanted. I have money and power. After we invalidate this charge that my rule is illegitimate, I can try and give you your own life. But right now, I need you, Carlotta. Will you help me?" his voice was mesmerizing.

Charley wanted to give him, well, everything. It was absurd! But still, she felt herself nod as he lowered himself so that his body hovered ever so slightly over hers. Like a big dark dream.

"I don't want your money or power," she spoke in a voice she hardly recognized.

It was happening so fast, like a force of nature. Charley wondered if she could still be dreaming. How could her body react so strongly to a stranger?

"Anything you want, I'll give you anything." *Mine. She's mine.*

"I don't care about that stuff, Rafe, I have no family."

"*Shhh*, it doesn't matter. I'll give you family, Carlotta. I'll give you anything. Just say yes, please, God, say yes."

Charley was captivated by his sudden vulnerability. *He needed her.* Nobody ever needed her before. She worked forty hours a week cutting cold cuts and scrubbing counters. It was a dead-end job, and she knew it.

After her grandfather passed away, Charley was

left alone in the world except for Buttercup. But this man, this gorgeous giant who believed he was a Wolf, *needed* her. She felt it.

"I'm sorry it has to be like this. So sorry, but I have to, they'll know if we don't, if I don't-," he whispered his words so close his breath mingled with hers.

Charley wanted to taste him. She wanted, she didn't know what, but oh yeah, she *wanted*. His lips brushed hers once, then twice. His tongue flicked out across her lips and she gasped.

"*Mmmm*, you taste like cherries," he groaned, and he kissed her again. This time his tongue dipped into her warm mouth and she opened for him with a soft moan.

"It's my Chapstick," she whispered.

"No, Carlotta, it's you," he licked her lips and kissed her again. He pulled back and she groaned her disappointment.

"I can't help this, I'm sorry. Your pheromones are so strong and with the moon this close, it's hard for me to stay in control. I *need* you. I'm sorry. Say yes," his voice rumbled, and Charley nodded.

"Yes, oh yes," she whispered.

Charley barely understood him, but she knew she was saying yes, and God help her she meant it too. The things he was doing to her were incredible. His

29

hands had an easy strength as he lifted her and peeled back the covers. Charley wanted more. She wanted him.

He pushed her gently onto the mattress and grazed her neck and chin lightly with his teeth. Charley clung to him, awash in a new kind of passionate haze she had never experienced before. His long hardness pressed against her thighs and he continued to lick and nip her mouth and neck while he undressed her.

She knew she should fight him. She should struggle to hold onto that virginity she had saved for the one man she would marry. But not even her twelve years of Catholic school could have prepared her for this onslaught of feeling.

How could she fight against something that felt *soooo* good? Why should she? It didn't matter. She still had to try, right?

"Oh God. Don't-," Charley's whisper was agonized. She moved her head from side to side against the soft pillow.

"Don't?" Rafe lifted his head, his blue eyes blazed as he fought to control himself.

"Don't-," Charley whispered again.

"Carlotta, do you want me to stop? Carlotta? -,"

"Don't, don't, oh, don't stop, please, oh please,

don't stop," she felt his relieved smile against her full breast.

"Thank God, oh, thank you," he breathed his reply and took her plump nipple into his mouth. A delighted gasp escaped her lips.

What was he doing? Tugging, sucking, licking, nipping. His tongue seemed to paint a picture across her body. She writhed under his expertise, wanting more. His hands left hot trails of desire along her taut body.

Charley's skin burned and Rafe seemed to know what she needed. He switched his attentions almost before she knew she wanted him to. Caressing, stroking, and squeezing her in ways she had never dreamed could happen to her.

Growing up with only an elderly grandfather hadn't left her much time for boys as a teenager. She attended Catholic high school, took some community college classes, and worked at Junior's part time. Then her grandfather discovered he had cancer.

She quit school, worked more hours at Junior's, and took care of him until he passed away two years ago. That brought her life up to date. She lived alone, with her cat. Worked, read books, and very rarely dated.

But here she was. A twenty-five-year-old virgin about to have sex for the first time ever with her kidnapper, who by the way thought he was a Were-wolf. *Whoa.*

Okay, she knew she'd have to deal with a whole lot of reality the minute she woke up from this night-mare/dream. She'd worry about it then. She'd even check herself into a mental health clinic just as soon as she got home. She'd do anything as long as he didn't stop what he was doing right then.

"I can smell your need, Carlotta, can you feel mine?" he pressed against her, his body hard and throbbing. She strained towards it like he was some goal she wanted desperately to achieve.

"Do you like this?" he growled and licked her with his tongue in long strokes from the tip of her rosy hard nipples down to her navel, and then lower to her inner thighs. She couldn't speak, she just moaned and gripped his hair in her hands. She left them there since he didn't seem to mind.

His hot breath hovered over her core and she flexed her hips instinctively. Charley couldn't think. She wanted something, *craved* something she couldn't describe. His big hands cupped her breasts as his teeth gripped the elastic of her white lace panties.

She felt a tug and knew they were gone. Ripped off with his teeth. *Oh my.* She felt his chest vibrate, a deep rumble as he slowly, reverently lowered his head.

His hands moved to part her. He *looked* at her, all

the while slowly stroking her thighs. Charley's mouth hung open. She couldn't believe what he was going to do. What she was going to *let* him do.

His eyes locked on hers as he lowered his mammoth head and kissed her there. Once, twice with his full lips. He looked up, gave her a carnal smile. His lips glistened with what she knew was her own moisture.

Then his long, thick tongue snaked out of his mouth and he *licked* her. The groan that escaped his throat rivaled her own. He lowered his head and lapped her. Sucking, licking, and nipping gently with his teeth.

Charley gasped and ground herself against his mouth shamelessly searching for something, some pinnacle she knew she had to reach. And then she did. White hot flames seemed to burst beneath her closed eyelids as he worshipped her body with his hands, his lips, and his tongue. She yelled her first ever release.

Rafe purred his contentment as he continued to suckle. *Slowly, soothingly*. She was lost in sensation as he changed position and removed his clothing.

Rafe needed her. *Now*. He cupped her buttocks, lifting her, and positioned his swollen head at her moist opening. He tensed and entered her slowly.

Charley felt him push inside of her. The sting was

brief, but the sense of connection, of communion, was strong. *Him, I've been waiting for him.*

"Carlotta," he murmured. He had to go slowly with her. He rubbed his finger in tiny, feather light circles, oh so gently, so tenderly over her throbbing sex.

Charley moved and Rafe sucked in a deep breath as he pushed even further inside of her. His eyes bore into hers. He needed to watch her as they joined. Her scent filled his nostrils, the Wolf in him demanded he claim her. *Now.*

"Rafe! Please," Charley thrusted upwards, but his large hands captured and stilled her.

"Easy, baby," he whispered and shifted. He cradled her gently in his arms and watched her every reaction as he fully pushed into her.

She felt him stretch her. Her soft body accommodated his pulsating strength. The tremendous rightness of it brought tears to Charley's eyes. She reached up and held his face as he filled her.

She pulled down his head. He allowed her to, his expression tense, until she kissed him. He groaned and opened for her. Her soft tongue tangled with his.

Rafe thought he would explode. For the first time, she initiated contact. He was completely at her mercy. He stilled and waited for her to command him. A Wolf always listened to his mate's desires.

Something inside of her must have known it too because she nipped his lip and pulled on his waist. He groaned aloud and thrust into her. *Mine.*

He pumped until her cries filled his ears. He growled and his hot seed filled her. Making her gasp. He had never felt so satisfied, so complete, as he did in that moment.

"Are you okay?" he trailed soft kisses down her throat and up to her mouth.

Charley could hardly believe what had just happened. It was better than anything she had ever read about. And she had read some mighty descriptive romance novels in her day. She kissed him back, loving the weight of him.

"*Mmm*, better than okay."

"Good, cause I'm not finished yet."

Rafe moved inside of her and she felt him swell instantly. Charley's eyes flew open.

"Is that supposed to happen so soon?"

"I'm a Werewolf. We heal quickly."

"Oh."

"But I don't think I could ever get my fill of you, sweet Carlotta," he breathed her name into her mouth as he joined with her.

Charley held on tight as Rafe drove her to the edge of sanity. He seemed to know exactly what she needed in ways she didn't know herself. *My destiny.*

Their bodies were slick with sweat. Rafe cradled her face in his big hands, kissing her as he sank into her welcoming warmth. She bit down just above his collar bone, gasping his name, and damn, if he didn't pump harder. Her spasms milked him, and he threw his head back, roaring his completion.

After what seemed like an eternity Charley opened her eyes. She was utterly spent, but not even exhaustion could stop the smile that spread across her face like sunshine.

Rafe moved down her body. His lips trailed soft kisses as he went. She missed his warmth. She wanted to pull him back on top of her. She should be ashamed, but shame was *not* how she felt. Not at all.

She watched as he tended her. Rafe's tongue snaked out and licked her thighs soothing her sensitized flesh. She couldn't move as she watched him. His dark head moved up and down as he ministered to her hot skin.

She wanted to hold her knees closed, suddenly embarrassed, but she had neither the strength nor the will to deny him. He parted her legs and looked at her with such reverence in his gaze that her heart skipped a beat.

She lay before him completely exposed. Charley sucked in a breath as he bent and licked away the remnants of her first time. He kissed her thighs then moved up ever so slowly to her most sensitive flesh. First, he tended her, then he moved with intent.

Charley gasped and arched off the bed. She undulated against his clever tongue. Her breathing grew heavy. Rafe knelt between her thighs and cocked his head to the side. She could feel the pressure build up in his powerful body as he waited for her response.

She reached up and grabbed his long hard length with both hands. His skin was like velvet. She cupped him and pumped him once, then twice. He threw his head back and groaned. A very satisfying sound. Charley bit her lip then placed his swollen head at her center.

"Are you sure I won't hurt you?"

"I'm sure, Rafe. I want this, I want you."

"*Mine*," he growled.

Charley moaned at the pleasure of him filling her. He was so strong. Hard, large, and sinewy. Like some sort of ancient warrior god.

Charley on the other hand, was soft and curvy. Her body full of dips and valleys. Her skin ivory to his bronze. Rafe kissed her full breasts, and she threw her head back, her hair cascading around her in wild disarray.

She never thought much about her looks. Never thought there was a reason to. She knew she was considered much larger than the norm. Advertisements and the media of the day continued to plaster pictures of ultra-skinny waif like models all over the place as the thing to aspire to.

Super-thin girls and women who were concerned with the size of their "thigh gap", a thing Charley could not possibly measure on herself as it was non-existent. She was always fond of food and when she was younger, she often felt bad about her weight. Dieting hadn't worked. She certainly wouldn't take pills or have surgery to fulfill society's standards of beauty.

In the 50s, she would have been perfect. But Charley couldn't complain. She was healthy, her yearly physicals stated as much. She had the odd date here and there. Guys in high school had told her she would be pretty if she lost some weight, but she shrugged them off and stuck to herself.

And she was glad. Now more than ever. She was in bed with a man who looked and moved like a god. And Rafe, well, he made her feel beautiful.

His expression was both fierce and humble as he traced lines along her collarbone, neck, and face with his long-fingered hands. He leaned down and kissed everywhere he had touched. Worshipping her with his mouth.

She met his lips and touched them tentatively with her tongue. Rafe had to work to control himself.

He could hardly believe her response to him. Could she really be his true mate? *Mine.* His Wolf growled inside of him and he gripped the pillow behind her head so hard it popped.

Down feathers flew around her head and she laughed. Rafe smiled too. *Beautiful.* Her scent, her taste, her passion, the waves of emotion that rolled off her, he'd take it all. She was his.

"You are beautiful," he nuzzled her neck just as she ran her nails down to his buttocks. And *squeezed.* His ability to think froze. He was insatiable, but only for her.

"*Grrr,* Carlotta, I don't think I can be gentle if you do things like that, you should stop," he growled in her ear. But his mate shook her head and squeezed harder.

"I don't need gentle, I need you," she wrapped her legs around his waist.

This was crazy. Charley knew it. *Later, I'll think later.* Right then she only wanted to feel. She waited her entire life to feel something half as real.

Rafe knelt in front of her, still joined he lifted her legs and put them on his shoulders, going even deeper inside of her. Charley gasped.

He ran his long fingers over her sensitive skin and moved. *More.* He seemed to sense her needs. When he moved inside of her it was like poetry.

Charley did the only thing she could think of. She held on and when she reached the height of their passion she cried out.

"Carlotta," he exhaled her name and Charley watched him as he exploded inside of her.

It was the most intimate moment of her life. Staring into the clear blue eyes of her very first lover. *Her only lover.*

They had made love. She may be a novice, but she knew this was more than sex. The way he looked at her in his moment of release melted away whatever protection she had built around her heart.

"Rafe, *mmm*," her voice sounded dreamlike and far away.

"Hey, baby, you hungry?" he cuddled her and kissed her shoulder.

"Actually, I think I'd like a shower," Charley felt around for her robe. Her cheeks burned. She couldn't quite meet his eyes.

Rafe wasn't having any of that. The last thing he wanted was for his new mate to feel shame after what they experienced together. He turned her head to face him, she had such beautiful brown eyes.

"Of course, but first I need you to hear something. I, I apologize."

Her heart stopped. Oh God! He was sorry they made love. She was shameless, having sex with her captor. And loving it! She was like elbows deep in Stockholm syndrome and *he* was *sorry*.

"No! Not that. I would never be sorry for making love with you, Carlotta. I'd never apologize for that," he growled, reading her mind again.

Charley didn't know what to think or feel as her heart resumed its steady beat, *bum-bum bum-bum*. Maybe he really was magical? It was uncanny the way he seemed to guess her every thought and emotion. Especially, when they were, *er*, in bed together.

She cleared her throat, her uncertainty growing. Everything was so strange and new with him, different from anything she ever experienced.

"What you gave me was a gift and I'll treasure it. Always. But that's why I need to apologize, for *not* being sorry."

Sorry for not being sorry? Well, that's new.

"Carlotta, my men took you without your permission and I just jumped you! I need to apologize for that. It's just that I can't because I am not the least bit sorry that you're here with me right now."

"Oh, thank God," she said and jumped into his arms.

Chapter Five

Rafe dressed then left to get food. He told her to wait for him inside the bedroom, but she was never one to take orders. After a quick shower, she searched his drawers for something to wear.

She found a pair of navy-blue boxer briefs and shrugged. They were the smallest thing in there, so on they went. She laughed as she caught sight of herself in the mirror.

Rafe was at least six feet two inches tall and over two hundred pounds. A good eight inches taller than her. Most of his clothes were going to be way too big. She kinda liked that.

She had to fold the boxers twice to get them to stay up. She topped off her ensemble with a flannel button down shirt. Of course, she had to roll up the sleeves half a dozen times to keep them from falling.

She knotted the shirt tails at her belly button since loose they reached down to her knees. Charley grinned as she braided her hair. *Guess I'm petite compared to someone after all. Take that Mrs. Gunfry!* She thought of her old gym teacher and smirked.

She tried the doorknob and was slightly surprised when it opened. The hallway before her was long and empty. It was certainly larger than any she had ever seen.

She knew she was in a house with eight men, one of whom she spent the last few hours making the most exquisite love with. There was also one other woman who lived there, *the sister*. But that was as far as she knew.

She counted ten doors from Rafe's room till she got to a huge staircase that looked like something out of Twelve Oaks from Gone with the Wind.

She looked around and was surprised at the quiet. *Hmm. Kitchen? Where is the kitchen?* She heard a noise. Like a blender. She followed it and opened the first door she found. *Eccola!*

Charley stood in a giant state of the art kitchen. The walls were painted a pale yellow. There were miles of marble countertops, polished wood cabinets, and stainless-steel appliances.

"Goddamn it, Seff! Did you use all the basil making those damned watermelon juice things again?" tall, beard boy shouted through a door opposite Charley.

She got a look at what he was doing. *Garlic, onions, peppers, tomatoes, basil.* He was trying to make sauce! She tuned out the argument and went to work.

Charley opened the large Subzero Wolfe refrigerator. She put back the peppers and onions and found some fresh basil in a plastic baggie in the veggie drawer. She pulled it out and handed it to beard boy who was standing behind her with his mouth hanging open.

"You know your herbs would last longer of you wrapped the stems in a damp paper towel. These baggies will make them mold and wilt."

She waited while he opened and closed his mouth like a fish out of water. Then he bent his head towards her and sniffed. Charley backed up instinctively. A ridiculously pleased smile broke out on his hairy face and he howled. *Like a Wolf.* Charley's mouth dropped open.

A stampede of men came into the kitchen and Charley felt like a fool. She stood there, half-naked, in front of her kidnappers and they were all smiles and pats on the back. *What the heck? Where was Rafe when she needed him?*

"Well, well, looks like we did good after all," said beard boy.

"Easy boys, you'll scare her. Hi, my name is Seff, uh, Seff McAllister. This here is Randall Graves," the soft-spoken blonde held out a hand. She shook it briefly. *These guys are not normal.*

They won't harm me. That she knew. They seemed to respect Rafe too much for that. Besides, they thought he was their leader. If only she could figure out the cause of this mass delusion.

"Okay, you still with me? The twins here are Kurt and Dib Lowell."

He pointed to the two red headed giants, then onto a tall thin male with a grim expression.

"This is Tate Nighthawk. Conall Truman, you'll remember. You, uh, gave him one hell of a bloody nose, and this is Liam. He's my baby brother."

They all nodded and smiled. Occasionally, they sniffed the air and grinned wickedly.

"Okay. I'm Charley, but I think you know that. Now I'm not saying I forgive you, but I am kind of hungry. So, Randall, what kind of sauce are you making?"

"The inedible kind," said Conall. He tried to duck out of the way, but he was too slow. Randall elbowed him hard in the gut. Tate winced, the twins snickered, and Liam bent over laughing.

"Hey man, you want to cook tonight? Be my guest! I'm a game developer, not a bloody chef!"

He threw his dish towel at Conall and stalked over to the mound of ingredients he had gathered.

"How about I help?" Charley grinned and followed him over to the counter where ingredients were strewn all over. The others followed, their expressions hopeful.

"She can cook?" someone asked.

"Put these away," Charley began sorting through the ingredients she wanted. She asked for a sauce pot and another for the pasta. She laughed as they rushed to do her bidding.

"Okay, for a simple meat sauce I am going to need a small piece of pork shoulder and maybe a beef rib bone or two?" They got her what she needed and watched as she taught not one, but seven males how to make a classic Neapolitan tomato sauce.

"What about staples, like sausage and meatballs?" Liam asked.

"Alright, we can make that too, but you guys are my sous chefs," Charley was no fool, after all she worked in a deli that catered. No way was she going to be chained to the stove in that massive house!

Twenty minutes later her enormous pot of sauce was simmering, an even bigger pot full of water laced with sea salt was just about to boil, and four dozen meatballs the size of softballs were in the oven. Randall was frying eggplant. Liam was chopping ingredients for a salad and Charley was rolling out dough for fresh garlic and herbed breadsticks.

Rafe entered the kitchen at a run, in his hand was a sack of fast food. "Has anyone seen Carl-," his stunned expression said it all. He dropped the fast food where he stood and grabbed her in a rough embrace which she happily returned.

"Hey, I'm okay," she stroked his hair back from his forehead and dropped a soft kiss on his lips. His eyes told her all she needed to know.

"Hey, boss, your mate can cook! Isn't that great!" said Liam from his position at the vegetable chopping block.

"You did all this?" he said as he sniffed the air and almost groaned from the delicious smells.

"Yeah, I was getting hungry, and I didn't know where you went."

"No, it's okay. I- Thank you."

She lifted the pan of breadsticks and placed it in the oven. Rafe smiled appreciatively as she bent over. He growled when he noticed Liam's interest and the young Wolf immediately turned his head elsewhere.

Charley lifted her head and looked at Rafe. *Was that a growl?* She must be imagining things.

"Okay, boys, I need you to set the table, get some

drinks, and grated cheese and we'll start bringing the dishes out in a few minutes."

Rafe was stunned at the way his mate took charge. *And just look at how his Wolf Guard fell into line!* He grinned like a madman. They were taking orders from this tiny woman, who just hours ago, was a prisoner. *Their* prisoner. Now, she was in control of everyone, and she completely took over his kitchen!

Rafe pulled out a chair for Charley next to his. He squeezed her hand and sat down to one of the best home cooked meals he had ever eaten. The rest of the Wolves waited for him to take the first bite. His eyes closed as he savored it.

His Guard smiled and dug in. They were a rowdy bunch, elbowing each other playfully and joshing around. Charley had never had any brothers, but if she could choose a family, she'd love one like this. Their jovial manner and goofing around put her at ease.

Rafe was just as casual in his mannerisms. It was obvious he was in charge, but the entire meal held a touch of informality that made Charley feel relaxed. She watched Rafe as he served himself another helping of pasta and four more meatballs.

He could really pack it away! And she thought they were crazy when they pulled out box after box of rigatoni.

Rafe was so ridiculously proud that his mate had made their meal that he couldn't stop grinning. That's when it hit him. She wasn't *really* his mate. He had promised to let her have her own life.

He stared at her as she laughed at one of Liam's jokes. *How could he let her go?* She looked gorgeous at his table with one leg tucked under the other, dipping a breadstick into her salad dressing. It was as if she were born to be his. And she got along with his Guard.

What if she wanted to leave? What if she demanded he keep his promise? His eyes narrowed. He knew there was no way he could live without her. His Wolf snarled in the back of his mind at the very thought of her out of his life. *Mine.*

After everyone ate their fill Charley stood up to clear the dishes, but Rafe stopped her with a hand on her shoulder. "No need for that, the guys will do it. We have a housekeeper who comes in the mornings. He takes care of things like the dishes, laundry, vacuuming..."

"He?"

"Oh, yeah. We are all for equal opportunity here."

"Really?" she looked at him with those big brown eyes of hers. He found it difficult to concentrate.

He could get lost in her eyes. He sensed her pulse

speed up and he watched as her lips parted. Rafe struggled to keep steady.

Chapter Six

She was beautiful with her long hair in a loose braid down her back, her straight nose, and full lips. Not to mention her figure. His body reacted just looking at her.

His mate had curves to fill his hands, a soft, flat belly, and rounded hips. Her legs were just long enough to wrap around his waist. *Sweet as honey*.

She had been innocent. A precious gift in this age. Now he wanted to growl at every male who looked at her. *Mine!*

Rafe shook his head. *Easy buddy. You'll scare her.* That was the last thing he wanted. His instinct was to protect and see she was cared for.

He knew in his heart she was his true mate, but he had to make her realize it too. That meant restraint. He'd give her some space. Let her see how good they were together.

"I have some work to do, but I picked up a few things for you when I went out. Some clothes and toiletries. Not that I mind seeing you in my clothes."

"That was thoughtful," her eyes rested on his mouth and Rafe swallowed. He hadn't felt like this since he was a pup.

"Um, would you like a tour of the house on your way back to our room?" Rafe wanted to punch himself in the face.

He sounded like an idiot. He saw the looks his Guard gave him. *Great. An audience.* He growled at a decibel Charley couldn't hear. The command unmistakable. *Back off.*

"I'd love it, thanks," Charley smiled. *Good.* He liked her smile.

They stood up and left the dining room. They made a quick detour to the laundry room off the kitchen where he swiped a pair of clean socks from his basket. He bent down and lifted her feet one at a time.

"So, your feet don't get cold."

"Thank you," her breathy answer told him more than her words. She had found the act of him dressing her as erotic as he had. He blinked to calm the beast inside of him that demanded he drag her into a dark room and have her again and again until she couldn't walk away from him. *Really enlightened thinking there, man!*

He stood up to put a little distance between them and started the tour. He showed her around several living/sitting rooms. The main kitchen she already saw, but there were smaller snack areas with fridges and microwaves. Werewolves tended to eat a lot.

There was also a game room, indoor and outdoor swimming pools, a hot tub, a gym, a weight room, a sauna, a ten-car garage with a working lift, fifteen bedrooms, each with its own bathroom and walk-in closet, a first aid room, a security room, a laundry room, two dining rooms, a ballroom, and a handful of offices.

Not to mention outdoor guest houses, poolside cabanas, and a huge fenced in garden with dense woods directly behind them. He also informed her it was a half hour ride to his private beach.

Fresh flowers graced the hallway. There were exotic potted plants everywhere. Lush and green, their fragrance was light and pleasant. The furniture was oversized and comfortable. Most of the rooms had their own working fireplaces and lots of natural light.

Rafe was conscientious and polite throughout the entire tour. A little too formal for Charley's tastes. At times, she felt self-conscious, but then he'd brush her hair back from her shoulder or take her hand, and everything was okay again.

"I think we should discuss our arrangement, Carlotta. On Christmas Eve, I will present you to my Pack representatives, including the elders, and you will be declared officially as my mate," he waited for her to react. This was so unfair. He felt like a jerk. Once he did that, she would be officially his.

"And then I'll go back to my life. That's what you said, I understand. One thing though," Charley bit her lower lip and looked up at the man in front of her. The man who in just a few hours changed her entire life.

"Yes?" Rafe tensed.

Please, don't let her ask me not to touch her again. He knew that wasn't going to happen. Werewolves were renowned for their virility. And his libido would go into automatic overdrive the minute she was officially matebonded to him.

"Can you bring me some of my clothes and Buttercup? My cat?"

Rafe couldn't help it, he lifted her up in a fierce hug. He laughed and squeezed her before placing her gently back on her feet.

"Of course! If you just make a list of what you need, I'll send Seff for you."

"Alright, thanks."

"I'll walk you back then I, uh, have work to do."

"It's ok, you go ahead, I'll find my way," she gave his hand a squeeze and turned to go.

Damn. He felt like a total piece of shit. His boys kidnapped her, literally. He practically forced himself on her, though seduce was the word he chose to employ. And yet she still agreed to help him out, even though he would totally get it if she wanted to drive a dagger through his back. And now, like a big dumb jerk, he had hurt her feelings. He could smell her sadness, it was kind of like moss and lemons, and it pained him.

He walked to his office feeling like crap. As he passed the huge Christmas tree on display in the main foyer he stopped. He would make it up to her, and he thought he knew how. He'd give her a Christmas she would never forget!

Chapter Seven

The first thing Charley did was head back to Rafe's bedroom. *Would it ever be ours?* Her thoughts wandered as she picked up the shopping bag he brought her and pulled out a pair of black lace panties, a matching bra, soft gray leggings and a jade green tunic style sweater. There were also fuzzy socks and a pair of black ankle boots.

After another quick shower, she dressed and reveled in how perfectly everything fit her. It was like he had memorized her exact proportions. Her cheeks burned when she recalled how he had gotten that information.

Charley strolled back towards the kitchen. She dug around and found a pad and blue ball point pen. Her favorite writing tool. She wrote down a list of what she wanted and went to look for Seff.

Instead, she found Randall. He was sitting on a big brown leather couch with an old acoustic guitar balanced in his arms. She watched as he strummed the instrument. He played with the ease of a professional. His eyebrows furrowed as he plucked the strings.

Charley smiled when she recognized the tune. *Bon Jovi*. A favorite of any born and bred Jersey girl. She was no exception.

She opened her mouth and hummed along with him. Randall perked up and nodded at her. She began to sing, and he slowed the tune down to match her style. He ended the song and went right into some Christmas music.

Charley sang along and loved every minute of it. After a few minutes, the room filled with the men of the house. Rafe was notably absent.

Charley didn't let that get her down. After all, he said he had work to do. They ended the set with a soft rock version of *Silent Night*. Applause and whistles filled the room. Seven pairs of curious eyes watched her as she grabbed a bottle of water and took a long pull.

"Damn girl, you got a nice set of pipes," Kurt, or maybe Dib, said and high fived her.

"Thanks, I was in choir back in school. My grandpa loved to sing carols around the tree. Randall is the one with the talent though!" She curtsied to her guitarist and he bowed back. A gentle smile on his face barely discernible through all the thick dark hair.

"Cool! So, you cook and sing, and the boss was smiling when he left. I think we picked the right one, huh, Seff?" Conall joined in, oblivious to all the groans and eye-rolls.

"Shut up, Con! Icsnay on the idnapkay!"

"Dude, for real?"

"It's okay guys. Despite being forcefully taken without my consent by you brutes, I, uh, I've worked out a deal with Rafe. I'll stay and help, then I get my life back. In the meantime, Seff, can you pick these up from my place?" she held out the piece of paper to him with hands that trembled ever so slightly.

Charley was once again dressed in Rafe's big flannel robe. She snuggled into it and ran a hand through her long damp hair. It was past midnight and Rafe still hadn't returned. It was ridiculous for her to feel abandoned, but she couldn't help it.

He didn't exactly choose her. His friends did. A gorgeous, important guy like him wouldn't choose someone like her. No family, no friends, no career. She was cute in her own way, but she knew she wasn't in his league.

Guys like him chose girls who wore a size 2 with

platinum blonde hair and frosty pink lipstick. Not short, chubby brunettes. Then there was the whole royalty thing. *Pack Alpha*. Whatever the hell that meant!

Werewolves, really? Maybe it was like an MC or gang thing? God, she hoped so. True, they were all big and good looking, and yes, they did tend to growl at each other. And, well, *during sex*, Rafe growled quite a bit. But was that normal for men? She didn't know. She had nothing to compare it to.

The doorknob clicked and Charley turned. She held a breath as he walked in. He looked startled to see her. His blue eyes wide as they looked her up and down.

"I thought you'd be asleep," his voice was gruff, like it was the first time he spoke in hours.

"Is that why you stayed away?"

"Yes. I, uh, didn't want you to feel like I was going to expect, you know, anything," he walked in and closed the door behind him.

"Look, for whatever reason earlier, we had sex. I'm not expecting you to force yourself to *be* with me. I'm your 'mate' for show, for this other guy to see, I get it. I can move to another room."

Quicker than she could blink he was across the room and kneeling in front of her. Charley backed up, surprised by his incredible speed. She almost slipped off the edge of the bed. He reached out and steadied her.

"Carlotta, believe me when I say that getting you into this mess was the last thing I would've wanted, but not because I had to force myself to be with you. That's the most ridiculous thing I've ever heard! Don't you know how beautiful you are?" he reached up and cupped her face. The look in his eyes made her want to believe him. No one had ever looked at her quite like that.

"I'm not beautiful, I'm cute," she replied softly, mesmerized by the depths of his blue eyes.

"Are you kidding me? With that long curly hair and those amazing brown eyes? And your skin? Soft and smooth and warm."

"I'm fat. And short," she moved out of his grasp and spoke matter-of-factly. Rafe's eyes bugged out of his head. And he pulled her back, so she had to look at him.

"What? Are you insane? Who told you that load of crap? Carlotta, you are beautiful. You look exactly as a woman should. You fill my hands perfectly, as *my* woman should."

"Rafe, I don't want to talk about my looks."

"Fine. Then let's discuss your courage, your brains, your talents as a chef and a singer, your passion, your strength, your heart, there are any number of things we can discuss that would clearly point out why anyone would be damn lucky to have you even look at them."

"How did you know I sing?" Charley looked at Rafe, uncertainty on her face.

Chapter Eight

U*h oh*. How was he going to explain this without sounding like a stalker? One thing for sure. He'd have to be honest.

Werewolves simply didn't lie. Living in a Pack made it impossible. When people lied, they gave off clues in their body language and their scent. As pups, they were taught to identify emotions and behaviors, so lying was not really an option.

"I heard you. I, uh, watched you. From my office. Common rooms have security cameras. I was just checking you were safe. Werewolves can be dangerous. Randall in particular. He plays music to soothe himself. When I saw you go in there I was concerned, but when I saw you open your mouth to sing, I just had to listen. It was beautiful, Carlotta. Just like everything else about you."

Technically, that was the truth, the rest he would keep to himself. For instance, he couldn't tell her that he followed her with his eyes as she walked from room to room. That he was becoming obsessed with her. That he had to stop himself at least a dozen times from getting up from his desk and taking her back to bed.

When he saw her approach Randall, one of his most dangerous wolves, he had jumped up ready to intervene. Then she sat down and began to sing. Rafe turned the audio on and had gotten the shock of his life.

Her voice was strong and soft, sexy as hell. When Dib high-fived her, Rafe had growled low and deep. Jealousy had almost overcome his reason. He had to use all his strength to deny the temptation to rip off Dib's offending hand.

It was no good being jealous and possessive. Besides, she wanted her old life when this was done. *No!*

Rafe wanted to change her mind. Hell, he needed to. In his heart, he knew his Wolf had claimed Carlotta. Letting her go was going to be damn impossible.

"Charley, call me Charley."

"No, I don't think so. Your name is Carlotta, *my* Carlotta," he dropped a whisper of a kiss on her mouth.

Oh yeah, this is what I've been missing. Charley thought as she tugged him closer. Her first experience with sex and she was a wanton! Insatiable and curious and gloriously wanton. *For him. Only for him.*

Rafe kissed her lips, lingering on her bottom one. He stood abruptly with her wrapped in his arms. That damn robe covered much too much! He placed her on the bed and tugged. It fell open and revealed her sublime nudity. He groaned as he looked his fill.

She was gorgeous, sensuous, and waiting, for *him*. With a low growl, he took off his clothes. He enjoyed watching her response. The catch in her throat, the way her eyes widened. He knew he was large and muscular. At first, he was afraid he'd frighten her, but the way her eyes ate him up let him know she liked what she saw.

He sniffed the air, and it was like a rush straight to his groin. She was ready. Rafe lowered himself slowly and carefully on top of her. Her body opened for him without prompting. His erection found its rightful place between her thighs.

"Slowly, I don't want to hurt you, baby," he had every intention of going slow, but Charley ran her hands down his backside and pulled.

She licked him from neck to jaw. Her lips found his as she wrapped her legs around him. He entered her slowly, closing his eyes tight as he tried to still himself.

She was like a drug to him. The more he got, the more he wanted. Yeah, but it was so much more than that too. She was like the air. He needed her that much.

Charley explored his back, chest and hips with nimble fingers. She squeezed with her legs and his control began to slip.

He nipped lightly at her neck and inside his mind's eye his Wolf came forward. Deep blue eyes glowing, Rafe raised his head and bit down, not to hurt her. To *mark* her. He sucked, *hard*.

She bucked underneath him, driving him closer to the edge. Rafe's chest rumbled with pride as Charley moaned his name. He was the first one to fill her, to taste her, to make her moan. And he was going to do it again.

"Rafe, I didn't ask before and it was foolish of me, but what about safe sex? Condoms?"

Rafe went still for a minute. He had just had the most mind-blowing sex of his life. *No, not sex. Love. They had made love.* He couldn't think straight. His heart was pounding, and his brain wasn't working yet. *The moon. She is calling.*

"Uh, Werewolves don't get sick like humans. Also, you're not ovulating. I'd smell it if you were."

She was beautiful in the afterglow of their love-making. He had explored every inch of her body. Her smell and taste would be forever ingrained on his heart and mind. How could it be that his Guard knew him so well? Whatever the reason, he was grateful.

"Sounds, *mm*, reasonable," she arched her back as he rubbed her stomach in gentle circles. It was the first time she didn't seem to doubt he was telling the truth. That was good.

Charley woke the next morning alone yet, deliciously sated. She blushed when she recalled all the things they had done during the night. She couldn't believe this was happening to her.

This may have all started out as a kidnapping, but it wasn't now. Hadn't been since she laid eyes on him. After all he never forbade her to leave. He simply asked her if she would stay.

And she said yes. For a while anyway. Charley wondered when it would happen. When would he ask her to leave? Wouldn't it be wonderful if it were true? If he really was a Werewolf and he wanted her to be his mate?

She yawned and stretched. Charley felt glorious. Like a new battery, completely charged. Rafe had mentioned something about his strength pouring into her, something called a *matebond*, but she had been too exhausted to listen.

The sound of something breaking and someone cursing made her lose her train of thought. She pulled on the green flannel robe and opened the bedroom door. Charley stifled her laugh at the sight before her.

"Goddamn cat! Get her!"

"Ouch! Oh fu-,"

A series of painful groans and furniture being knocked down followed. Charley knew the problem immediately. Seff held his neck. Red blood ran through his fingers as he tried to get his breath back. Randall was holding an equally bloody scratch on his forearm and Conall was on the floor.

She watched as he tried to wrangle the one and only Buttercup out from under an accent table. Pieces of the broken porcelain vase, fresh cut flowers, and accent marbles were everywhere. Water soaked the carpet and dripped over the side of the table. *Uh oh.*

"Meow!" Buttercup ran and leapt straight into Charley's arms.

"Hey, baby, my little Buttercup, my sweetie," she cooed and stroked the cat's fur. She raised an eyebrow at the three grown men sprawled all over the place.

"Sorry, guys, I should have mentioned he doesn't like strangers. Oh, can you bring up my bags please. Thanks."

"Oh, he doesn't like strangers! Thanks for telling

us that! Could have used a little warning," Conall mumbled as he, Randall, and Seff hefted her suitcases, kitty toys, and one freshly cleaned, bright blue litter box up the stairs.

Charley hid a smile at all their grumbling. Served them right! She had them leave the litterbox in the hall. She set Buttercup down and watched him get acclimated to his surroundings.

"Wait, you're going to let that beast roam the place?"

"That's right. You got a problem with that?"

Seff stopped Conall with one hand up, "No, ma'am, we do not. We apologize if we were out of line. Not used to cats, you know. Werewolf thing and all," he bowed. Randall and Conall followed suit.

"If it's okay with you, ma'am, I'd like to go over some things for the meeting when you are ready? You will need to know how to conduct yourself around the rest of the Wolf Pack and our *guests*, ma'am, if that is okay?" Seff's formality made Charley smile.

So, they were really going to treat her like the whole Alpha female thing, huh. Okay then. Maybe she should take a moment to clear her head. She went inside and began to unpack. Humming thoughtfully to herself.

The walk-in closet was huge, but a space had been made for her belongings. When she opened her bags, she realized they had packed much more than just some of her things.

She hung up a few items and left everything else in her suitcases. After all, her time there would be short. Unless, well, she'd think about that later.

Chapter Nine

Charley rifled through the kitchen. Rafe was in his office and she needed to think. Cooking had always been therapeutic for her, especially when she had a problem. And boy did she ever! *Hmmm, chef salad sounds good.* She got out some fresh produce, a dozen eggs, fresh cheese, and cold cuts.

A couple dozen cheddar drop biscuits and home-made honey mustard vinaigrette would complete the meal. Charley set up her ingredients, sighed, and got started.

Everything she could ever want was right in front of her. And not just inside the kitchen of her dreams, but Rafe, and the others too. She walked over to the extra-large double sink and rinsed her hands. Oh, the

Christmas breakfast she could prepare here! Charley smiled.

She and her grandfather always made a large breakfast to celebrate Christmas Day. It was the one tradition she kept since his passing. Though nowadays it mostly consisted of a single pancake, citrus fruit salad, and a strip of uncured bacon. It was no fun cooking just for yourself.

Maybe she could make some quick cookies for after lunch too? She quickly prepared a batch of butter-cookie dough and was not surprised to find a cookie press and sprinkles in the cabinets. She smiled as she quickly prepared a sheet of her favorite Christmas cookie. Tree shaped with red and green sugar crystals. Just how she liked them.

Her hands moved automatically as Charley thought about what was important to her. She had always wanted to get married and raise a family. In her daydreams, she was the mom who stayed home to raise her children. She'd make them cookies and treats and help them with homework. She'd be there for them.

Maybe it was because her grandpa was her only parent and he had worked long days to keep her in private school. He did his best and she loved him, but she had spent a lot of time with strangers or in after school programs.

She disliked the ideas of daycares and nannies. If she were married to a man like Rafe, he could easily provide her with the security and stability to stay with the kids. *Wait, where the heck did that thought come from?*

She shook her head and winced. No one mentioned marriage. True, she didn't ask to come here, but she never felt so at home before. This place, these men, felt like they were *hers* in a way.

They were polite, funny, incredibly courteous, and sweet. Like the brothers she never had. Then there was Rafe. He was truly one of a kind. A gentle and generous lover. Gracious, intelligent, and he had an air about him that commanded attention.

An innate power that was subtle, yet undeniably strong. Her heart beat faster just thinking of the big guy. Heavy footfalls fell behind her and she straightened her back. *Rafe.*

"Hey," he walked up to her, placed big hands on her hips and kissed her neck. Charley almost dropped her knife. She leaned back into him, eyes closed.

"I'm sorry I had to leave you this morning. There was something I needed to attend to. *Mmm*, smells good."

"Thanks. I guess I missed breakfast. I made enough for everyone."

"I meant you, but the food smells great too. You know, you don't have to do that."

"*Mmm*, I know, but I like to cook."

More footfalls, some sniffing, then groans of pleasure.

"Oh my God, are you making us lunch?" Dib or Kurt said. They both sniffed the air, identical looks of ecstasy on their faces.

"Oh, thou fairest maiden, Charley! Wilt thou honor me as my personal chef forever unto eternity," Liam dropped to his knees at her feet.

"Beat it, pup," growled Rafe, only half kidding.

"Alright, alright, come on, boys, go wash your hands and set the table. Lunch is in ten minutes."

They howled and ran for the lower floor bathrooms. Shoving each other like twelve-year old kids.

"My God, you'd think they never saw food! Animals!" Rafe shook his head and went back to nuzzling her neck.

"Pardon my frankness, but none of you look like you never saw food. And, *mmm*, Rafe unless you want one of my fingers in the salad you better stop that now or I'm afraid I'll cut myself," he stepped back immediately. Charley missed his warmth.

"I'd never let a single hair on your head be hurt," he vowed.

"Good to know. Please carry this inside," she nodded at the pitcher of vinaigrette and the two giant bowls of salad. He dropped a kiss on her temple and picked up the food easily in his big hands.

She took the cookies and biscuits out of the oven. She scooped the warm, golden biscuits into bread baskets and placed the cookies aside. Charley put the baskets on the dining table and was surprised to see no one eating.

"Isn't it alright?" she had used plenty of cold cuts, cheeses and hard-boiled eggs.

"It's perfect, darling, we were just waiting for you," Rafe pulled out the chair to his right.

"Thanks," Charley sat awkwardly and waited, but no one moved. She reached for the salad and was surprised when Rafe took the tongs from her and filled her plate. He filled his next and passed the dish to Seff. He did the same with the dressing and biscuits.

He surprised her even further by taking her hand and saying a brief grace over the meal. Charley had to blink back tears. They were all being so respectful, so kind. *For her*.

Conversation started and soon they were joking and talking about the upcoming holidays. Charley laughed with real joy as the guys ribbed each other. The front door opened, and she heard a female voice.

"Hello? Anyone home? Hey, is that food?" in walked the tallest, most beautiful woman Charley had ever seen. She was thin, toned, and had long wavy blonde hair.

She had a gym bag slung over one shoulder. A badge on her hip and a gun. Fresh snow dusted clothes and hair, giving her a sort of fresh glow. Charley's eyebrows rose.

"Oh, hey! How you doin'? You were passed out last time I saw you and you had less on," at Charley's blush the woman winked. She dropped her bag, grabbed a plate and helped herself. The men seemed at ease with her except for Tate who ignored her completely.

"Jeez, Cat, slow down. Let me introduce you. Carlotta, this is Catriona, my baby sister," Rafe said with an indulgent grin on his face.

"I'm sorry, are you a police officer?" asked Charley.

"Macconwood Sheriff's department, actually, I'm a deputy. Nice to meet you, officially."

"Well, that's just great! *You*, you're sworn to uphold the law? Congratulations, *officer*, you're an accomplice to a kidnapping!" the room got very quiet.

Everyone averted their eyes except for Rafe and

Cat, who met Charley's glare. She averted her eyes and shrugged her shoulders.

"You know, Charley, you don't look like you're being held against your will. Besides Pack comes first," she dug into her salad.

"Oh, so you're delusional too then. Great, just great!" Charley stood up hands on her hips and walked over to Cat.

"Carlotta, we can talk about this later. Besides, you agreed to stay."

"Yeah, but not when your sister undressed me. Hey, I'm talking to you, at least look at me! You had no right! As a woman and a deputy, you should have done *something*. Well, what do you have to say for yourself, young lady?"

Catriona stopped eating and stood up to her full height. Not backing down a step, Charley stood toe to toe with her and stared her directly in the eye. Cat dropped her gaze first. Even before she heard Rafe's warning growl.

"I apologize, ma'am," she grinned and bowed to Charley before reseating herself and taking another bite.

"Hey brother, I like her. Try not to fuck it up," Cat said in a not so whisper to Rafe. In fact, all the Guard seemed to watch Charley with admiration in their eyes.

Charley looked at each of the stunned faces at the table and sat back down next to Rafe. Her posture was stiff, displaying her annoyance, but her heartbeat was normal. Rafe let out a relieved breath. *Yes*, he thought, *I have clearly chosen well*.

"Well, eat!" she commanded, and they did.

Chapter Ten

After lunch Rafe took Charley on a tour of the grounds. It was the first time she saw the house from outside. It took her breath away.

Maccon Manor was a veritable fortress. Big and foreboding, like a castle in a fairytale, made of stone and iron. There were state of the art security fences, cameras, and even a manned gate. Rafe pointed each one out to her. Her safety his foremost priority.

He needed her to see that he could provide protection. For her *and* any future young. *Easy.* He needed to curb all thoughts of any children.

The very idea of her bearing his child made him want to take her, right there on the ground. He looked over the fine form of his mate as she bent down to pick up a pebble. *Damn.* She was beautiful.

Charley appreciated the natural stone walkways and the meticulous landscaping. There were luscious evergreens adorned with twinkle lights and shrubberies surrounded by smooth pebbles that reflected the light like glass. They were sure to be spectacular come spring.

Someone must lovingly tend all this, she thought absently. Rafe held her hand but didn't pull or drag her. He was patient with her questions. And she listened with interest as he explained about the history of Maccon, NJ and its ties to his family.

"There has been a Maccon running Pack business in this area since the first settlers. About five generations back. You see, Werewolves live longer than humans and as a result so do their human mates. We can be killed, but it's difficult. I must tell you that we do have enemies, Carlotta, dangerous enemies. But I swear, I'd die defending you."

Charley didn't know how to react. She cared for Rafe, heck, she might even love him. But how could she help him with this delusion of his when everyone seemed to feed it?

She reached up and caressed his jaw. She knew he meant that part about risking his life for her. She didn't doubt that.

"Carlotta, this rogue Wolf, Skoll, wants me out of the picture. As Alpha, I will always be a target for my enemies. It's important you know I can protect you."

"Rafe, this delusion, isn't real."

"But it *is*. You must understand as a Werewolf I *can't* lie."

"What does that even mean? You gonna burst into flame or something if you fib?" Charley tried to joke, but it sounded lame even to her ears.

"No. Different emotions, different states of being have scents. Basically, I can smell a lie and so can other Werewolves. I must be *matebonded* by Christmas Eve. I know I promised to give you your own life, but first you must mate me. Will you?"

"I thought we did already," Charley blushed and Rafe reacted predictably. He wanted her, so very badly.

"I'll cherish our intimacy always, Carlotta, and I'll never be able to thank you enough for the gift of you, but I need more. I need you to formally marry me."

Charley's heart pounded in her chest. She placed a hand over her belly. Could this be her one chance for her dreams to come true? *A husband, a home, family.*

"Of course, you wouldn't have to stay."

Rafe's voice was low, and Charley felt her stomach tighten. She disliked the idea of their *having* to marry. She wanted to be wanted, to be loved. But maybe she was being greedy.

"Look, I said I would help you, Rafe, and I will. I don't know about all this supernatural stuff, but I believe you believe it. And whatever *this* is between us, I gave you my word."

"So, you will?"

She nodded. Whatever fantasy he believed, it seemed like maybe this would help him resolve some problem. And honestly, she just wanted to be as close to him as she could for as long as possible.

Her insides melted as his face lit up. He grabbed her in a tight hug and swung her around. Kissing her desperately on the lips. Charley clung to him. She felt her legs go weak just as he lifted his head.

"I have the paperwork in my office. Will you come with me now and sign? Then Seff can perform the ceremony. He's licensed to perform marriages."

"You want to do this now?" she looked down at herself. She knew if she left his side even for a minute, her brain would take over and reason would never allow her to go through with it. Charley looked into Rafe's blue eyes. Was she really willing to marry a virtual stranger? She inhaled and nodded her head. There was no backing down now.

Half an hour later she was legally married, in a pair of old worn jeans and a yellow sweater. Rafe held her left hand up and slipped a perfect blue sapphire the size of a nickel onto her ring finger. It was set in a thick platinum band carved with what Charley thought looked like runes.

"It's a star sapphire, the ring of the Alpha female of the Macconwood Pack. It belonged to my ancestors, Eoghan and Ailis," Rafe's voice was deep, and Charley held his gaze. One by one, his Guard entered the room and knelt before them.

"I place this ring on your finger and proclaim to all under my domain that you, Carlotta Marie Palmieri Maccon, are the Macconwood Female Alpha and my mate *semper et in saecula*," he kissed her hand and knelt at her feet. The moment seemed to last as Charley felt a sort of warm vibe spread throughout her body.

She didn't know what was happening. One minute it was all legalities, *one, two, three* and they were married. Then, as if by magic, all the guys in the house and Cat appeared and Rafe said things she couldn't possibly fully understand.

"Holy shit," someone murmured.

"Ooof!"

"Shhh!"

Charley ignored everyone except Rafe. Her new husband's eyes were glowing. His expression intense, he was focused solely on her.

"Come, let's leave them."

"You mean, like, now?"

"*Shhhh*, go!"

Charley ignored the footfalls in the background. Great vibrations were coming from Rafe's throat and hitting her right between her thighs. The door shut and before she knew it, they were alone, and he was on her. Right where she wanted him to be.

His dark brown hair was carelessly brushed back from his face. His blue eyes glowed a shade darker than usual and in them Charley saw heat, desire, and power. In two moves he was completely naked before her. A perfect male specimen.

He was bronzed and muscled with dark curling hair that began on his chest and trailed downwards. Charley's eyes widened. He had thick legs corded with muscles. They stood apart and she was drawn to where he was most masculine. His chest heaved with the force of his breathing. He was beautiful.

Charley felt her own breath quicken as he moved in closer. His nimble hands made quick work of her clothing, then he reached for her hair. He gently pulled her tresses free from the ponytail she had worn all day. He leaned in and Charley gasped as he licked her from neck to nipple.

He had to bend to get close enough, his height so much greater than hers, but he didn't seem to mind.

He lifted her onto his desk and laid her back, licking and sucking as he went. He lavished attention on her breasts and belly. Rafe couldn't get enough of the sweet taste of her skin. He knelt before her and parted her supple thighs.

Rafe's growl started deep in his chest sending vibrations straight through to her core. Charley squirmed in his hands as he leaned forward. His fingers smoothed up her legs and he parted her skin to reveal her most secret place. His breath heated her, she pulled him by his thick hair, but he was immovable. Desire burned through her body. *She needed him.*

His growl grew louder and soon he was kissing her swollen flesh. His tongue delved inside, darting and probing. He rubbed his cheeks against her sensitized thighs. Every touch, every sound, and sensation seemed amplified in the closed quarters of his office, but Charley could no more stop her moans than she could his soul shattering touch. *Why would she want to?*

Rafe held her gently in place with his large hands while he suckled her. She was all honey and cherries and Rafe was greedy for her. He kept at her, licking and kissing, using his fingers and even his teeth, until Charley almost bucked off the desk. Her groans echoed all around him and he felt his own sex grow long and hard. Rafe's body quivered in anticipation. He wasn't prepared for his baser reaction to her complete submission.

The Wolf inside of him was howling and he knew without a doubt this woman was his mate. His destiny. His world. He would do anything for her. He would kill for her. Even die for her. *How would he ever let her go?*

Lightning surges of pleasure shot through Charley's body. She was close. Rafe scented her arousal and pleasure, heck, he *felt* them. It was like her body was calling out in a frequency that only his could answer and it was glorious. It almost brought him to his knees.

Rafe stood, his clothing a careless heap on the floor. They moaned in unison as his engorged sex came into her with a single perfect thrust. He fought for control, but nothing he had ever learned or experienced could have prepared him for the sensation of bonding with his mate on this level. It was beyond all previous notions and expectations.

Charley loved having his weight on top of her. Thick and hard, yet smooth and soft as velvet, he filled her on so many levels. Every kiss, every touch, the slightest movement of his body, the tiniest growl that emanated from his chest, sent her closer to the edge of ecstasy. She had never felt as complete as when he swept her away in his most intimate embrace.

He thrusted into her welcoming heat and Charley knew that nothing could ever be that perfect. Nothing would ever compare to these moments. She cried out, an agonizing moan, as they reached the height of their pleasure, together.

Charley snuggled into Rafe's warm chest as he carried her through the empty hallway as if she weighed nothing. Wrapped in his soft sweater with her clothes piled on top of her he managed to make her feel like a princess. Albeit a princess who had just engaged in some deliciously naughty desk sex.

She smiled and sighed, a satisfied sound. He nuzzled her head as he walked. His steps strong and steady, his voice deep and husky.

"I'm sorry I couldn't wait until we were upstairs. I should have had more control," he seemed shaken, maybe embarrassed.

Charley reached up and stroked his cheek. There was more hair than there was just an hour ago. He looked scruffy and handsome. His lips were slightly swollen, and she felt her cheeks heat as she recalled how they had gotten that way.

"S'okay, I couldn't wait either," she bit her bottom lip as he opened the door to his room and placed her on the duvet. He smoothed a stray curl away from her flushed face and kissed her lips.

Chapter Eleven

"**H**ow do you feel, *my Carlotta?*" Rafe's hand grazed her neck, his fingers stroked her softly. He couldn't stop touching her. He had no desire to.

"Mmm, good. What time is it?" Charley felt a little sleepy, but good. So very good. *How could this be real?* She wondered if it was possible for a person, *for her*, to truly be this happy.

"Eight-thirty, baby, no, no don't move," he held her down gently when she tried to sit up.

"It's later than I thought, I should make dinner."

"Don't worry about it. The guys ordered a bunch of pizzas. Are you hungry?" Rafe asked. She shook her head as he bent and kissed her softly.

"Carlotta, tonight is the full moon."

Charley stiffened. Time for the truth. He had to come clean about this whole Werewolf nonsense.

"Rafe, I—"

"Please, just listen. You are my female, my mate, you're protected. Do not be afraid. Our matebond will be complete after tonight," he spoke matter-of-factly. His ice blue eyes held a faraway look and for the first time, Charley felt uncomfortable. She didn't know how to respond. *Poor delusional man.* Tears sprang to her eyes.

"Oh Rafe, you are *not* a Werewolf. Maybe we can get you some help?"

"Trust in me. I beg you. I am a Werewolf. Even if you want to leave after, I need you to understand this is not a delusion. I'm so sorry I didn't have the strength to send you away in the beginning, I just couldn't, one look and I knew you were my destiny," he ran his hand through his hair. Charley thought she saw him tremble.

"My Guard is sworn to protect you now. Just remember, I would die before I let anything hurt you. Don't be afraid."

He drew open the floor length curtains revealing the French doors that led to the terrace. He opened them too, letting the frigid night air creep into the bedroom. He didn't seem bothered by it even in his nudity. *A few more minutes and the moon would be completely full.*

"Whatever you're thinking, please, please know this, I love you, Carlotta."

Big, soggy tears ran down her face as she tried to hold in her sobs. She had waited her whole life to hear those words. What was she going to do when nothing happened? How would she console him?

"Don't worry, sweet, you'll be safe. I swear it. After the Change, I'll stay with you awhile, then I'll have to go," he bent and touched her forehead with his own.

"Don't worry, my love. The Pack has to see their Alpha, but Cat will stay behind to keep an eye out," his head still touching hers he leaned down and licked the tears off her face and neck. She wanted to hold him, to keep him there. But he backed away from her embrace.

He turned his head toward the terrace, a look of anticipation and bliss on his face. That's when Charley noticed the moon. Beautiful, bright and completely full. Its rays seemed to land right on Rafe, encompassing his entire body in an unearthly glow.

Suddenly the air around him shimmered. His breathing increased. He started to sweat, and his entire body vibrated. He was just so large and powerfully built. More muscular than any man she had ever seen. *Beautiful*.

He mouthed something to her. She thought it was, *I love you*. Three words. That's all they were. She thought she had imagined them moments ago, but here he was confirming what she thought was delusion.

Charley sat up on the bed, wrapped in a sheet and watched as the man she had married mere hours ago seemed to shimmer in and out of the moonlight. *I love you*, fitting words for this moment of magic and myth. She wished she could return them, but she was struck dumb by the sight before her.

Rafe's brown hair darkened to a deep blue black. Then suddenly, it wasn't hair, but more like fur and it ran down his arms, his hard belly, and legs. His large human body doubled over. Rafe grunted and groaned. He seemed to be in pain.

Oh my God, Charley ran to help, but Rafe seemed to melt right before her eyes. Where he had been crouched down on the ground only moments before stood a black Wolf the size of a small pony. Charley stopped so suddenly she fell flat on her butt.

The Wolf looked at her. His chest was heavily muscled. His paws massive with long, sharp claws. His eyes were a darker blue, but they were full of knowledge and recognition. Charley crouched down in front of him and stretched out her hand as tears rolled down her face. *A Werewolf! It was all true!*

The Wolf held still as she approached. Unsure of herself, she wiped her face and bent her head down, beneath his. It seemed right somehow.

He walked to her and wrapped his great Wolf body around hers. Heat emanated from him, as well as, strength and power. Charley reached out with shaky hands and stroked his fur. It was smooth and silky, but underneath his body was hard and muscular.

His huge Wolf tongue hung out to the side as she scratched behind his ear. Charley's laughter rang throughout the room when Rafe went belly up like a great big puppy. She couldn't believe her eyes. Fear took a backseat, replaced by wonder and amazement. *A real, live Werewolf! And he was her husband. For however long he wanted her.*

He stood up suddenly, jarring her from her thoughts. He walked over to the terrace and barked. Then he looked over at her then back down to the yard. Charley stood up and went to him wrapped in nothing but a sheet from the bed. It trailed behind her like the train of a wedding dress, and she felt like something out of a dream.

She peered over the railing at the eight magnificent Wolves that were gathered below them. They were all huge, bigger than the average Wolf, but none quite as large as her Rafe. They sat on their haunches and howled into the night air when they saw them both together.

Charley made out a dark brown one with long shaggy fur, *Randall*; a light buff one with short smooth fur, *Seff*; a golden one with shorter fur that spiked into a ridge on his back, *Conall*; a smaller, paler blonde one that could only be Cat; a black one with a scar that zigzagged across his shoulders, *Tate*; two large bright red wolves, the twins *Dib* and *Kurt*; and a snow-white wolf, *Liam*. They were a stunning group. As Wolves or humans.

Charley felt a force, a power almost like the hum of a generator, soar through her body. Suddenly she felt as if she were connected to them all. She could feel their presence touching her heart and mind. Rafe stood out among all of them. His heart the clearest. His love for her strong and pure.

Her chest heaved as the force of that power filled her. All her life she had felt alone, especially after her grandfather passed, but not now. All she felt now was love for this man, this Wolf, who had filled her empty life as no one else ever could.

More Werewolves approached from the dense woods behind the manor. They seemed to be acknowledging her, their new Alpha female. Charley felt her heart swell with pride and wonder.

She turned as Rafe's claws made a clicking sound on the beautiful wrought iron fence that surrounded the terrace. He watched the display with a regal air about him. He acknowledged his Pack with a short howl then turned to her.

"Thank you," Charley said to him, her left hand over her heart, "thank you so much."

His great Wolf head was cocked to the side as he dropped down to his paws and approached her. He licked her hand gently, a soft whine escaping his jaws.

"No, I'm happy. I really am. You're beautiful. All of you," surprised and delighted she wrapped her arms around his furry neck, and he nuzzled hers back.

Rafe gently stepped back from her and she released him. Then he leapt in front of her, blocking her view. She heard the clacking of claws on the stone tiles. A Wolf had apparently jumped up, though they were at least two stories high.

Rafe growled once and Charley noticed it was Cat. The female Wolf lowered herself into a submissive position. She approached Charley and sat down at her feet. Charley steeled her nerves and reached out to rub the female between her pointed ears.

She could not afford to be afraid. In truth, she was more curious anyway. Her musings stopped when Cat's sandpaper-like tongue snaked out and licked

Charley's hand. She grinned at the She-Wolf. They would be just fine.

Cat will stay with you, Rafe's voice whispered in her mind. Charley nodded and wiped her eye as her husband barked once then vaulted over the terrace. He landed soundlessly on the frozen grass below.

She walked over to the French doors and closed them, though she wanted nothing more than to watch. She tried listening for them, but only managed to hear a few distant howls. Cat, on the other hand, seemed to hear things Charley's human ears couldn't pick up.

"So, what do I do now?" Charley mused.

Cat walked to the closet and nudged the door. Charley opened it and watched the Wolf pull a night-gown from a hangar gently with her mouth.

"Maybe you're right, a shower first, then bed."

Charley indulged in a long hot shower. She brushed her damp hair and donned the nightgown Cat had chosen for her. It was soft and practical. She shrugged and went to snuggle in bed. Cat was lying down on the rug. She couldn't tell if the Wolf was asleep or not, but she suspected she was trying to make it easier for Charley by not moving around so much.

Sometime later Rafe came back. She knew him instantly. It was as if her soul recognized his. She opened the terrace doors in her soft cotton nightgown and Cat flew out of them just as Rafe stepped inside.

It was ridiculous to wish she were in silk and lace instead of worn cotton, but she couldn't help it. It was her wedding night, after all. She wanted to be beautiful for him.

As if sensing her mood, he licked her hands gently and nuzzled her belly. Then he leapt up on the huge bed. Charley joined him. She wondered at the idea that she was in bed with a Werewolf. Silk or not, she was with him now and that was all that mattered. It was everything.

She must have dozed off while staring at Rafe. *Her husband. Her Wolf.* She was awake now and the male wrapped around her was all warm skin and hard muscle. And he was happy to see her, judging from the hardness she felt rubbing up against her bottom. She pushed back into him and smiled at his groan.

Next thing she knew, her nightgown was off, and she was up on her knees with him behind her. He gently eased her head down and spread her thighs. She sucked in a breath, more than ready.

Rafe parted her slick flesh with his hands. She expected him to take her hard and heavy. Moisture flooded between her legs as she anticipated how he would fill her. She gasped aloud when his rough tongue found her instead. Charley moaned and rocked back against him as two fingers joined his tongue and entered her from behind.

His thumb circled her most sensitive flesh then his mouth was back, lapping at her. She felt deliciously exposed. Like she had never been before anyone. *For him, only him.*

His chest rumbled against her and she could almost see his smile. A now familiar heat coiled low in her belly. It was a delicious secret the way her body opened for him and only him. She wanted more than his mouth. She tossed her head from side to side gripping the pillow in front of her as she almost lost control.

"Rafe, I want to feel you inside me when it happens."

Then his mouth and hands were gone, and he pushed his long erection into her with a deep groan escaping his lips. He kissed her neck as he went in and out, in a rhythm as familiar as breathing. They spiraled together, he plunging, she pushing back into him. Charley groaned his name as pleasure skyrocketed throughout her body.

Rafe could hardly breathe as her contractions milked him for everything he was worth. *My God*, she was something else. *His mate*. He should never have told her he was going to let her go. There was just no way.

She was part of him now. Part of his heart. He had to make her see that. Being with her like this eased a fear inside of him he didn't even realize he had. Happiness was not something an Alpha Wolf counted on. Duty and tradition were more the norm. But now, *with her*, it was a definite possibility.

His world was different from hers. Packs had rules. His parents were no love match. Mated by contract at birth, destined to control the Macconwood Pack. Theirs was a cold union.

His mother bore him out of duty. His father was slightly better. He took the time to teach Rafe how to be pack Alpha, but little else. After his mother's infidelity yielded his little sister, she fled the manor and left both pups to his father's bitterness.

Rafe had never dared dream his life could be different. He rejected the idea of a betrothal contract, but he knew he'd have to mate one day for his heir. He never thought he'd find a soulmate. Certainly not in a spunky human woman. One whom his Guard happened to kidnap.

He wished he'd seen her first. Met her in a normal setting, courted her, made her fall in love with him. Well, he'd just have to make her see she was his. His mate, in every sense of the word.

He knew it in her scent, he felt it in the vibrations that came from her luscious body when they were together, and he tasted it on the salty sweetness of her skin. Rafe kissed her shoulder as he withdrew from her. He tucked her against him as they regained their breath together. She was his everything. *Mine*.

Chapter Twelve

"M mm, morning," Charley said as she opened her chocolate brown eyes to meet the icy blue ones of her husband. He laughed and kissed her curly head.

"Good morning, my sweet mate."

"Rafe?"

"Yes," he stopped breathing. Would she ask to leave now that she had seen the truth? Charley sat up, her eyes grew dark and contemplative.

"Rafe, I want to apologize," he exhaled as she spoke. Relief coursed through his veins. *She wasn't leaving. Not yet.*

"You were telling the truth. I didn't believe you and you were telling the truth. I am sorry for that and

I have so many questions for you, I don't know where to start."

"Anything. You can ask me anything," he clasped her hands in his. He brought them to his mouth and kissed her palms. *God*, he loved her scent. Like honey and something else that was all her.

"Is it painful? When you change?"

"Not anymore. The first few times are rough, Werewolves can only change after puberty and are weak in the beginning, but with time our strength grows, and the pain goes away."

"When you're a Wolf how can you understand me?"

"It doesn't happen with everyone. Abilities differ from Wolf to Wolf. As we are mated, I expected to be able to understand your feelings, I admit I was surprised to understand your words perfectly."

"*Mm.* I heard you too, when you said Cat would stay with me, but it was only after that hum that I felt. The one that like, connected me to all of you. How did you do that, anyway?"

"What do you mean?"

"Well, when I saw you, all of you, it was like when you turn on a generator or go past power lines and electricity is in the air. Well, I felt that, but it went through me and then you were all here. In my mind and my heart. I could feel you."

"Carlotta, I've heard whispers of this, legends really, but never in my wildest dreams."

Rafe's heart stopped for a minute then swelled. She was amazing. He reached for her beautiful face with his hands, then he kissed her.

Tugging on her bottom lip as she wrapped her arms around him. He shuddered with pleasure as she embraced him.

"You're a wonder, my Carlotta. If my recollection of our legends is accurate, you're what we call a *whisperer*. Randall would know more. He is sort of our keeper of legends. That's why he invented that game of his, *WolfMoon*."

"*WolfMoon*, really? I had friends from school who played that!"

"Lots of humans do. He's made the Pack a fortune with it. Most of the money is his of course, but I did front him the funds to start so I own a percentage of his company."

"Wow!"

"I know, right?"

"So, from every movie or book I've ever heard about Werewolves are cursed men. Is that true?"

"Yes and no. Our curse is not that we turn into Wolves. Our curse is that we are kept from our Wolves. We can only merge with them at the Full moon, but that may change now."

"How?"

"There is a group within the European Packs, the *Hounds of God*. Within their circles is an American Werewolf, a teenage girl, she lives here, in New Jersey. Her name is Grazi Kelly. It's possible she can break this curse. It's vital to our survival as a species."

"That's a lot of responsibility for a teenager, but if she lives here, isn't she part of your Pack?"

"Well, that's tricky. She's the Greyback Pack heir, but I have afforded her the protection of Macconwood."

"Okay, sounds reasonable. What about this other Werewolf, this Skoll who wants to hurt you?"

"Don't worry about Skoll, I'll handle him."

He felt her stiffen and rubbed her back. The idea of her even saying the name Skoll sent rage coursing through his veins. He would shred that bastard Wolf if he even looked at his mate.

"When is the meeting with the council?"

"Christmas Eve."

"Well then, we better get started."

Charley spent the next few days going over Werewolf etiquette with Seff, getting to know the rest of the Wolves, and spending endless hours alone with Rafe. He was tender, kind, and always willing to explain things she didn't understand about Pack life.

She always did her best thinking when she

cooked, so when she was trying to get through her what-to-do what-not-to-do lessons with Seff, they worked in the kitchen. That afternoon she was preparing a huge roast beef. Seff practically drooled the entire time they spoke.

"What are you doing now?" he asked while going over his list of notes.

"Well, I'm rubbing olive oil onto the meat before I put on my *secret* seasoning. Just kidding, don't look so sad! It's really just Kosher salt and fresh ground black pepper. The olive oil will help the meat seal in its juices when it gets into the hot oven. You want to flash it with intense heat then lower it for about two hours. That way it will be tender, juicy and rare."

Seff growled with anticipation. He cleared his throat, obviously ashamed of himself. Charley just laughed. These guys were always eating. It amazed her how fit they were.

She looked down as Buttercup walked by, fluffing his tail at her as he went. Her cat was certainly more at home amongst a Wolf Pack than she could have ever expected. She hid a smile as Seff backed away from the creature a snarl on his face.

"Don't you worry Seff, I already guessed you guys are big meat eaters that's why I'm making three roasts," Charley laughed again as he refocused on the meat and ignored the cat.

"Now, what does it mean to be Alpha female?"

"Well, you are second only to Rafe. You must never put yourself in a position of submission to anyone except him. No bowing or lowering your eyes. You see Werewolves are very aware of body language. You can and should make eye contact with everyone. You're the Alpha female, it is proper for all of us to shift our eyes after three seconds. No more, no less."

"Okay."

"This is important. Never look away first. Try to think of everyone as a potential threat. Werewolves are notoriously territorial. Rafe wouldn't hesitate to tear someone's throat out if they dared disrespect you. As his female and a human, he will be very protective. It is proper."

"Well, I've been taking care of myself for quite some time now."

"Yes, but not under these circumstances. Remember everything you do will reflect on Rafe. The last thing we need is for him to look weak or foolish. Please Charley, you must listen to what I'm telling you. Our stability, heck, our *survival* depends on it."

Charley nodded at him. This was serious business. At her signal Seff lifted the heavy tray into the oven. He slid it onto the rack, and she closed the door.

"I would never do anything to hurt Rafe. Ever."

"I believe you," Seff nodded his head.

"I'm sorry we brought all this down on you. You know the kidnapping and everything. If you still want to leave after the meeting, I'll do everything I can to help."

"Thank you, Seff. For the apology, but I think I may end up thanking you for everything else too," she blushed and began peeling carrots, potatoes, and onions. Her skilled hands moved quickly as she put the veggies in a dish with salt, pepper, and olive oil. After everything was in the oven, she set the timer and grabbed her notes.

Charley found herself alone at the table going over what she had learned. After an hour of instructions, Seff bowed and left her to review. The meeting as it turned out was more of a formal party.

Complete with gowns and tuxes. A seamstress had come earlier in the day with a selection of gowns for her. As a sneakers and jeans kinda gal, it was something of a revelation.

She chose a strapless silk gown in a pale blue that fell to the floor. It hugged her curves in all the right places and ended with a small flair at her feet. The dress was lovely, reminiscent of the 1940s. The color was the perfect backdrop for her ring and would remind everyone of her status. She had chosen it with great care.

Chapter Thirteen

That was the easy part. The hard part was the list of rules Seff had given her. *Never lower your head to anyone in the room. Never look away first. Never allow yourself to be touched first. Keep pace with Rafe. Follow his lead.*

It was the way they recognized her higher position in the Pack. Rafe was the only one higher than her. She would be seated on his right side. Seff would be on his left. She learned he was the pack's Beta or second in command. Randall was third.

All the Wolves who shared the house were actually an elite group of warriors, handpicked by the Alpha. They were charged with keeping Pack business running smoothly and alerting the Alpha to any problems or new occurrences. Like this business with that teenage Wolf and the foreign Pack. It had huge implications, Seff told her.

Rafe spoke a little about this, but she had no idea the vastness of his reach. There was so much going on in the world that she never could have guessed. *How could she?* She worked at a deli. Her grandfather had been in the army and told her a little about the evil that existed in the world, but to think there was a constant supernatural battle going on was incredible.

"Did you find something you liked?"

Charley's heart thundered in her chest as Rafe spoke from just behind her. She turned and met his gaze. Heat, desire and genuine concern shown in his eyes. His emotions as clear as her own. How could she *not* have fallen for this man? This Werewolf? And she had fallen, so deeply in love with him that she was willing to leave everything she knew to be a part of his world.

"Yes."

"That's good. Did Seff go over things? Is there anything you want to review?"

"Is it true that no one is allowed to touch me? That is unless you permit it. No shaking hands? No kisses on the cheek?"

He answered her question with a nod.

"I don't understand. That sounds very, um—"

"Strange? Not really. I'm the Alpha. My mate is

mine to protect. Anyone who dared touch you without my permission in a formal setting would be indirectly challenging me."

"What if it happens? What if someone does want to challenge you and uses me to do it?" fear gripped her heart. She knew Rafe needed a mate to hold his position. It was the reason for her abduction after all. But she could not bear to think her presence could possibly cause him harm.

"Don't worry, love," he embraced her.

Charley breathed in the woodsy scent of him and clung. She would have never guessed in a million years that she could feel this way about another person. The thought of harm coming to him was enough to stop her heart cold. Her one hope now was that she would be able to fulfill her role as perfectly as Rafe had filled her heart.

The night of the party came quickly. Too quickly for Charley's peace of mind. She walked down the grand staircase in the most luxurious dress she had ever worn in her entire life. She felt as though she was suspended in a kind of dream. *Magical.*

They were all there at the bottom, waiting for her. Dressed in their custom-tailored tuxes, the men of the house looked gorgeous. But no one lit a candle to Rafe.

He was taller and bigger than all of them. At his

throat was a star sapphire pin that matched her ring. Charley's heart pounded and her breath caught. *I love him.*

The moment he saw her, their gazes locked. Electricity sizzled between them. Rafe's eyes traced her from the top of her gently swept up curls to the tip of her high heeled toes. He inhaled and extended his arm.

"You look beautiful," he murmured as she placed her hand just above his elbow. She didn't notice seven heads bowed in deference to her, nor the broad smiles that came from a few of them. She couldn't tear her gaze away from him.

Rafe kissed her free hand. Approval and something more in his gaze. Charley felt power radiating off him. He looked regal, but there was more to it. He seemed to ooze dominance.

"Thank you, Rafe, you look beautiful too," her breath caught as he smiled at her. She felt her pulse speed up and her heart pounded like mad as love for this man warmed her from the inside out.

The ballroom was decorated for the season and filled to the brim with people. *Wolves,* Charley guessed. Everyone was dressed to the nines. There were tables laden with fine food and champagne. Real holly boughs and pine garland with large blue velvet bows graced the posts and walls. White poinsettias and roses sat elegantly on every table.

Charley blinked back happy tears. A twelve-foot Christmas tree sat in one corner and was completely decorated in blue and silver ornaments. The star on top was a brilliantly lit. It was beautiful. Music played softly in the background, but no one danced.

Charley's gaze was drawn to a tall man by the far wall. He was surrounded by four men. He had dark hair pulled back into a ponytail and he wore a black on black suit. His eyes looked furious when he saw them. Charley moved a step closer to Rafe.

That man looked cruel and dangerous. *Skoll*, she thought. She looked at her husband and her unease was immediately laid to rest. Charley and Rafe stepped into the room together, as one. The music stopped and a man stepped to the microphone.

"Members of the Macconwood Pack and honored guests, it is our pleasure to introduce our Alpha, Rafe Maccon and his bride, Carlotta Maccon."

The room erupted in applause as they entered surrounded by the seven Wolves whom Charley now thought of as brothers. She walked beside Rafe to the center of the dance floor.

Seff had explained this part to her. Like a traditional wedding reception, Rafe and Charley were to open the dance floor together for the first time as husband and wife. She was more than ready. She had dreamed about this moment her entire life.

"Okay?" his blue eyes bore into hers and Charley forgot everyone else in the room. They moved in perfect time with the band.

A violinist stepped forward and Charley couldn't stop smiling. Rafe swirled her and danced her around the room. When the song ended, he leaned in and pressed a kiss to her lips to another outburst of applause.

He led her to the head table where he stood by her side. Together they greeted their guests. Charley had never seen anything like it. No one moved to touch her hand or kiss her cheek. They simply smiled and offered their congratulations.

A group of older men came to them first. They were all handsome in a Sean Connery sort of way and Charley smiled at the approval in their eyes. She held herself erect and followed Rafe's lead.

"This is my mate, Carlotta. Darling, these are the Pack elders, Stephen Dark, Carl Warren, and Devon Blake," Rafe introduced them, and Charley kept her eyes level.

"Congratulations, dear boy. We'll see the documents later," Stephen spoke, and they bowed in turn.

They left, but the procession was just beginning. Rafe clapped his male Packmates on the back, offered the women a smile and a word. Conall and Liam accepted gifts for them, Seff and Randall flanked the couple, and the rest of the Guard stood behind.

The greetings and well wishes went on forever, but Charley smiled through it all. It was as if she was born to fill this role. She had just accepted a glass of water from Seff when she felt her husband tense.

Chapter Fourteen

Skoll and his men walked towards them. He moved with the slimy gait of a snake rather than a Wolf. His slick backed hair reminded Charley of those 1980s drug cartel movies. Who the heck did this guy think he was? Rafe straightened to his full height. Charley held herself perfectly still.

"Ah, well, it seems you have found a *wife* after all. Well, isn't that just grand. Tell me, you didn't happen to kidnap her by any chance did you, Rafe?" his lightly accented voice reached Charley's ears.

Skoll was huge, but Rafe was bigger still. He met Skoll's stare and after too long a moment the other Wolf looked away. He seemed to grind his teeth as he bared his throat slightly. Rafe growled, a threatening sound, nothing like Charley had heard before.

Coming from anyone else she would have been terrified, but she only felt pride that it was her husband.

"I've brought a gift, for the bride," Skoll snapped his fingers, and a pair of hands held a wrapped box out to Charley.

His sinister gaze met hers, but when she didn't back down, he lowered his eyes and thrust the box forward again. Randall stepped forward, took the box from Skoll, and snapped his jaws. His teeth gleamed white from behind his long hair and beard.

"My mate and I thank you for attending our wedding party, Skoll, perhaps now your *concerns* are put to rest, but just in case they aren't, I am happy to take this up in an official arena with you," Rafe's voice had taken on a timbre Charley had never heard before.

"Oh, I doubt your human bride would appreciate a quarrel on her wedding night."

"On the contrary, I believe my *mate* would suit just fine."

Charley wanted to hold Rafe back, but she remained still, a bored expression on her face. Seff had warned her of this. The best thing she could do was appear unaffected.

A contest of wills seemed to be taking place right in front of her and Charley had nothing to do but wait it out. Seff had explained about posturing and respect. What he hadn't told her was seconds would feel like hours as the two Wolves faced down. Rafe was clearly better at intimidation for the simple reason that he was the more dominant Wolf.

"That won't be necessary, *Alpha*, after all, it is a party, gentlemen, madam," Skoll bowed his head again and walked away, his men trailing behind him.

Rafe remained on alert until he was far away from where Charley and the rest of his Guard stood. He made a mental note to have that gift brought to his office for inspection. He didn't want anything that had touched Skoll to come near his mate.

The rest of the night passed in relative ease. Charley laughed and talked. She danced to the amazing band with Rafe, and then with others after she approved of them.

She ate the wonderful delicacies before her and reveled in the holiday spirit that seemed to be with everyone. It had been so long since she had really celebrated Christmas. She felt like Cinderella at the ball, only better. Several of the Pack females were introduced to her by Cat, who wore a gorgeous silver sequined dress.

Charley noticed some tension between her and Tate, but she ignored it. Hopefully, after she got to know her better Rafe's sister would confide in her. After all, she was her sister now too. That made Charley smile even brighter. *If only things were permanent.* Doubts crept into her mind and she pushed them away. *Not tonight.*

The moment came when Rafe and the elders left the room to have their meeting to disprove Skoll's claims that his rule was illegitimate. Seff followed his Alpha armed with the paperwork that would prove their marriage, but still Charley worried. *What if it wasn't enough? Would he have to fight?*

Later that night, still dressed in her gown Charley stepped out onto the bedroom terrace. It was Christmas Eve. Snow fell softly from the night sky, drenching the yard in pure virgin white. Like a dream.

The party was over, the guests had left, and Rafe was still in his meeting. Buttercup circled her feet a few times before retreating to the fireplace. He seemed to like this home full of Werewolves. So, did she. *If only he had asked her to stay.*

She turned and went to the closet. Tears rolled down her face as she got out her suitcases and began throwing her clothes inside of them. She was sure by now that Rafe would have suggested their temporary situation be made more permanent.

Maybe he didn't mean it when he said he loved her?

Charley sobbed softly and tried to zipper the suitcase through tear filled eyes. She didn't hear the door open. Nor did she notice the sight of her husband, horrified at what he saw.

"Carlotta?" Rafe's heart pounded in his chest. It sounded loud as thunder to his sensitive ears. *He was too late. She was leaving.*

"No, no, I'm sorry, you, you told me it wasn't permanent. I guess, I just thought—"

Charley stopped and hid her face in her hands. She was so ashamed of herself. She wasn't one to beg, but for this man she just might.

Rafe dropped the large, wrapped box he held and fell to his knees in front of her. He reached for her hands and gently pulled them from her face.

"Please, Carlotta, I know my world is crazy and scary and different from anything you ever knew, and I would change it all for you if I could. Please don't cry, and please, don't leave. Don't leave me."

Charley gasped. More tears fell. Rafe didn't know what to do. *Did he offend her?* He held his breath, then she threw her arms around his neck and kissed his face. He exhaled and tightened his grip.

"You don't want me to go?" Charley asked.

"Of course, I don't want you to go! Look, look here," he picked her up and brought her to where he dropped the large, wrapped box. He nudged her gently until she tore at the paper.

Inside was a large basket with the name *Buttercup* inscribed on a gold plate that hung from a blue velvet ribbon. There was even a huge fluffy white bed to go inside.

"You see, I even got the little demon his own bed," Rafe nudged Charley with his head and Charley laughed and then cried some more. She hugged Rafe and kissed him again as his arms encircled her and brought her fully against him.

"Stay. Please. Always."

"Wild horses couldn't drag me away, Rafe."

"I love you, Carlotta. I love you so much," his voice grew husky as he held onto her.

"I love you too."

They kissed and undressed each other right there on the floor. Rafe grabbed the comforter and placed her on top of it. Then he touched his hot skin to hers, careful not to hurt her. He kissed her from the top of her head down to her toes.

Their joining was a slow and deliberate union unlike any they had shared. They kissed, and tasted, squeezed and caressed each other, careful not to miss a single inch. He loved her and she him until the soft rays of sunlight crept into the room and touched them both. It was the best Christmas she ever had. Well, so far.

Charley's Wolf. Her mate. For life.

The end.

Liked this story? Don't stop now! You can read all of the Macconwood Pack Novel Series here, and don't forget the Tales! Happy Reading... Awooooooooo!

Beware... Here Be Dragons!

The Falk Clan Tales began as my stories surrounding four dragon Brothers and how they find their one true mates, but when a long lost brother arrives on the scene, followed by a few more Shifters...what can I say? The more the merrier!

Each Dragon's chest is marked with his rose, the magical link to his heart and his magic. They each have a matching gemstone to go with it.

She's given up on love. But he's just begun.

In The Dragon's Valentine we meet the eldest Falk brother, Callius. He is on a mission to find a Castle and his one true mate, one he can trust with his diamond rose....

C.D. GORRI

His heart is frozen. Can she change his mind about love?

In The Dragon's Christmas Gift our attention shifts to Alexsander, the youngest brother of the four. He has resigned himself to a life alone, until he meets *her*.

Some wounds run deep. Can a Dragon's heart be unbroken?

The Dragon's Heart is the story of Edric Falk who has vowed never to love again, but that changes when he meets his feisty mate, Joselyn Curacao.

She just wants a little fun. He's looking for a lifetime.

We finally meet Nikolai Falk and his sexy Shifter mate in The Dragon's Secret.

She doesn't believe in fairytales, until a Dragon comes knocking on her door.

Meet Castor Falk, the long lost brother of our original four Dragons, and his sassy mate Josette. The Dragon's Treasure is full of adventure and laughs.

Nothing can surprise this six hundred-year-old Dragon, except maybe her.

Devine Graystone meets his match in Sunny Daye, an irrepressible Wolf Shifter with a heart of gold. Read their story in The Dragon's Surprise.

He's a hardcore realist until she dares him to dream.

Nicholas Gravestone doesn't know what to think when he spies Minerva Lykos on the property his Dragon covets. Can this unlikely pair come to a truce? Find out in The Dragon's Dream.

Thanks for reading.

xoxo,

C.D.

*Dragon Mates & Dragon Mates 2 boxed sets are now available in hardcover, paperback, and ebook. *Get a discount when you buy direct!*

Have you met the Barvale Clan Bears?

Looking for a Paranormal Romance series that is loads of growly fun?

Meet the Barvale Clan first in the Bear Claw Tales! A complete shifter romance series about 4 brothers who discover and need to win their fated mates!

Titles are:
Bearly Breathing
Bearly There
Bearly Tamed
Bearly Mated

Followed by two more spin off series, the Barvale Clan Tales, featuring:

Polar Opposites
Polar Outbreak
Polar Compound
Polar Curve

and, of course, the Barvale Holiday Tales, beginning
with A Bear For Christmas
Hers to Bear
Thank You Beary Much
Bearing Gifts
Bearly Friends!

*Look for more of these sexy, heartwarming holiday inspired
tales soon!*

*No cliffhangers. Steamy PNR fun.
Get a discount when you buy direct from my store.*

Go and read your next happily ever after today!

Other Titles by C.D. Gorri

The Dragon's Christmas Gift: A Falk Clan Novel 2

The Dragon's Heart: A Falk Clan Novel 3

The Dragon's Secret: A Falk Clan Novel 4

The Dragon's Treasure: A Falk Clan Novel 5

The Dragon's Surprise: A Falk Clan Novel 6

The Dragon's Dream: A Falk Clan Novel 7

Dragon Mates: The Falk Clan Series Boxed Set Books 1-4

Dragon Mates 2: The Falk Clan Series Boxed Set Books 5-7

The Bear Claw Tales:

Bearly Breathing: A Bear Claw Tale 1

Bearly There: A Bear Claw Tale 2

Bearly Tamed: A Bear Claw Tale 3

Bearly Mated: A Bear Claw Tale 4

Also available in a boxed set:

The Complete Bear Claw Tales (Books 1-4)

The Barvale Clan Tales:

Polar Opposites: The Barvale Clan Tales 1

Polar Outbreak: The Barvale Clan Tales 2

Polar Compound: A Barvale Clan Tale 3

Polar Curve: A Barvale Clan Tale 4

Also available in a boxed set:

The Barvale Clan Tales (Books 1-4)

Barvale Holiday Tales:

A Bear For Christmas

Hers To Bear

Thank You Beary Much

Bearing Gifts

Bearly Friends

Also available in a boxed set:

The Barvale Holiday Tales (Books 1-3)

Purely Paranormal Romance Books:

Marked by the Devil: Purely Paranormal Romance Books

Mated to the Dragon King: Purely Paranormal Romance Books

Claimed by the Demon: Purely Paranormal Romance Books

Christmas with a Devil, a Dragon King, & a Demon: Purely Paranormal Romance Books

Vampire Lover: Purely Paranormal Romance Books

Grizzly Lover: Purely Paranormal Romance Books

Christmas With Her Chupacabra: Purely Paranormal Romance Books

Purely Paranormal Romance Books Anthology Volume 1

The Wardens of Terra:

Bound by Air: The Wardens of Terra Book 1

Star Kissed: A Wardens of Terra Short

Waterlocked: The Wardens of Terra Book 2

Moon Kissed: A Wardens of Terra Short

*Now in a boxed set and in audio!

The Maverick Pride Tales:

Purrfectly Mated

Purrfectly Kissed

Purrfectly Trapped

Purrfectly Caught

Purrfectly Naughty

Purrfectly Bound

Purrfectly Paired

Purrfectly Timed

Dire Wolf Mates:

Shake That Sass

Breaking Sass

Pinch of Sass

Kickin' Sass

Love That Sass

Wyvern Protection Unit:

Gift Wrapped Protector: WPU 1

Tempted By Her Protector: WPU 2

Alien Protector: WPU 3

Unexpected Protector: WPU4

Jersey Sure Shifters/EveL Worlds:

Chinchilla and the Devil: A FUCN'A Book

Sammi and the Jersey Bull: A FUCN'A Book

Mouse and the Ball: A FUCN'A Book

Chicken and the Paparazzi: A FUCN'A Book

Jersey Sure Shifters Books 1-3 anthology

The Guardians of Chaos:

Wolf Shield: Guardians of Chaos Book1

Dragon Shield: Guardians of Chaos Book 2

Stallion Shield: Guardians of Chaos Book 3

Panther Shield: Guardians of Chaos 4

Witch Shield: Guardians of Chaos 5

Vampire Shield: Guardians of Chaos 6

Guardians of Chaos Volume 1 Books 1-3

Guardians of Chaos Volume 2 Books 4-6

Twice Mated Tales

Doubly Claimed

Doubly Bound

Doubly Tied

Twice Mated Tales Anthology

Hearts of Stone Series

Shifter Mountain: Hearts of Stone 1

Shifter City: Hearts of Stone 2

Shifter Village: Hearts of Stone 3

Hearts of Stone Books 1-3 Anthology

Accidentally Undead Series

Moongate Island Tales

Moongate Island Mate

Moongate Island Christmas Claim

Mated in Hope Falls

Speed Dating with the Denizens of the Underworld

Ash: Speed Dating with the Denizens of Underworld

Arachne: Speed Dating with the Denizens of Underworld

Asterion: Speed Dating with the Denizens of Underworld

Hungry Fur Love

Hungry Like Her Wolf: Magic and Mayhem Universe

Hungry For Her Bear: Magic and Mayhem Universe

Hungry As Her Python: Magic and Mayhem Universe

Island Stripe Pride

The Tiger King's Christmas Bride

Claiming His Virgin Mate

Tiger Claimed

Tiger Denied

Tiger Rejected

*Tiger Tales Anthology Books 1-3

NYC Shifter Tales

Cuff Linked

Sealed Fate

Virtue Saved

A Howlin' Good Fairytale Retelling

Sweet As Candy

Standalones:

The Enforcer

Blood Song: A Sanguinem Council Book

Spring Fling (co-written with P. Mattern)

Witch Shifter Clan

The Hybrid Assassin

###

Coming Soon:

Purrfectly F*cked

If The Shoe Fits: A Howlin' Good Fairytale Retelling

Thrilled By Her Protector: WPU 5

Blood Witch: Witches of Westwood Academy

Spirit Witch: Witches of Westwood Academy

Fire Wolf: Witch Shifter Clan 1

Snow Fox: Witch Shifter Clan 2

River Dragon: Witch Shifter Clan 3

His Carrot Her Muffin (featured in the Eat Your Heart
Out Holiday Anthology)

###

Young Adult/Urban Fantasy Books

The Grazi Kelly Novel Series

Wolf Moon: A Grazi Kelly Novel Book 1

Hunter Moon: A Grazi Kelly Novel Book 2

Rebel Moon: A Grazi Kelly Novel Book 3

Winter Moon: A Grazi Kelly Novel Book 4

Chasing The Moon: A Grazi Kelly Short 5

Blood Moon: A Grazi Kelly Novel 6

*Get all 6 books NOW AVAILABLE IN A BOXED SET:

The Complete Grazi Kelly Novel Series

The Angela Tanner Files

Casting Magic: The Angela Tanner Files 1

Keeping Magic: The Angela Tanner Files 2

*The Angela Tanner Files Paperback 2 Book omnibus

G'Witches Magical Mysteries Series

Co-written with P. Mattern

G'Witches

G'Witches 2: The Harpy Harbinger

G'Witches 3: Summoning Secrets

Witches of Westwood Academy

Co-written with Gina Kincade

Water Witch

Air Witch

Fire Witch

Earth Witch

Excerpt from Sealed Fate

I t was snowing, but that wasn't new. Konstantin huddled beneath the broken concrete and waited for the big men to leave. He'd heard the shouting from all the way down the street when he'd gone to pick up his little sister, Alina, from her ballet lessons.

Though his family was poor, Papa and Mama sacrificed much so she could learn to dance. Konstantin was proud of his sister's already budding talent at just six years old. She'd been a surprise to the older couple whose son was already a teenager, but they all doted on her.

Konstantin was almost old enough to work the docks with his father, but Mama insisted he finish school. At nearly seven feet tall and still growing, it was proving difficult to remain unnoticed by the local bratva. That was something his mother feared more than anything.

"Be a good boy, Konstantin. Stay away from the gangs, and criminals," she'd told often him.

After all, it was his dealings with the local crime bosses that had left his Papa with a permanent limp and physical disabilities from the multiple toes and fingers that were missing from his feet and hands. Shifters could recover from many wounds and injuries, but not amputations. That was something even their enhanced healing abilities could not overcome.

The screams got louder, and Konstantin picked up Alina who'd just started to cry. The sounds were coming from the building where his family rented an apartment from Ivanovich. The head of the local bratva had many slums on the city where he took advantage of the many poor Shifter families.

His inner beast scratched and roared, but he was no match for the many members of the bratva waiting for their boss outside. Instead of facing them and risking Alina's life, he covered her mouth with his hands and hid them both in the cellar of the neighboring building.

The old man was yelling about missing rents and late payments. He was going to use Konstantin's father as an example, or worse, take it out on his mother. That was something, he could not allow.

"Alina, will you stay here? Hidden for me, yes?" he asked his baby sister.

Blue eyes clear as the sky looked up at him, swimming with tears. She nodded her head, already older than her six years and he nodded, cursing roughly under his breath. He prayed he was not too late.

By the time he reached the apartment the men were gone, and his mother was wailing over the prone body of his father. Papa was gone. Killed by the bastards who ruled over all of them.

"Konstantin!" she cried, standing up and going to him, still covered in her mate's blood. "You must run. Go to your Uncle. Je will put you on a ship---"

"What about you? Alina?"

"Where is she?"

"In the basement next door. Let me get her," he said, frantic with worry.

"Yes, get her. I will pack."

When he once again returned to the apartment, he found the neighbors gathered. They shook their heads and turned their backs on him and his family, shunning them even as his father's body grew cold on their kitchen floor. Anger surged, but his mother was there, stopping it before he could blow like a steam engine.

"Come. Now. There is no time," she said, handing him a suitcase and taking the whimpering child from his arms.

They ran through the street, ducking in alleys, and moving faster then the humans around them. Tiger Shifters had night vision and traversing through the ice slicked alleys was quick work for them. They reached his Uncle's house in no time at all.

"You've come," Uncle Petyr said, grabbing his sister in a quick hug.

The man took his niece and handed her off to his wife who cuddled the child close. All the adults were trying not to cry, but Konstantin could feel their grief. Shared it with them.

"Can you get him out of here?" Mama begged.

"Only the boy. I am sorry," Uncle Petyr said.

"It is good. he will make a good life and we will come later," she said, nodding. "Okay Konstantin? Yes?"

"I want to stay with you," he said, a boy's dream.

"No, I won't let them have you too," Mama cred, holding him tight to her breast. "I love you son, but I need you to live. Here, there is only death waiting for you. Now go. Be strong. Be the man I know you can be. We will be together one day."

"We go now," Uncle Petyr said, grabbing the suit-case and taking Konstantin's hand.

"Mama? Mama!"

"Come now, boy. Be quiet or you will bring those monsters here."

That fact shut him up faster than if his Uncle had slapped him. Konstantin looked one last time at his mother and sister, who'd returned to her side. He waved and nodded, biting back his own tears, then he left his Uncle's apartment. And Russia.

And he never looked back.

Grab the rest of the story here: https://www. cdgorri.com/books/sealed-fate

Excerpt from Bearly Friends

❄❆❄

The wedding reception finished around two in the morning, and Betty had about all the fun she could stand.

Always a bridesmaid, she thought with misery as she pulled on the hem of the stupid short, neon green dress she and seven other unfortunate females had to wear as part of Nancy Freehold's wedding party. Betty did not even know why she was asked to be in the wedding, even though Nancy was technically her third cousin.

They'd gone to Barvale High together, even graduated the same year, but they hardly spoke. Betty was too much of a geek for most people. She spent her weekends watching reruns on the SYFY or talking to her houseplants.

Even her Bear was annoyed at her lack of love for

adventure, but she couldn't help it. Betty was a realist. Even if she was a Shifter, that didn't mean she was the outdoorsy type. Quite the contrary, in fact. Give her a laptop and a Big Gulp, and Betty could entertain herself for hours.

"Hey Betty! Leaving already?" Melinda Ora, another bridesmaid, and Betty's second cousin, was giggling up a storm as she rushed out onto the veranda overlooking the parking lot where Betty was walking.

"Yeah, I'm done," Betty said, grinning at her. "You staying for last call?"

"Yeah, um, something like that," Melinda replied, her attention diverted to the big male who'd stalked her outside.

"There you are, girl. I thought we were gonna dance," a familiar voice said.

Betty froze as the big male cozied up behind Melinda, bending his wavy dark head to sniff at her neck, while he whispered something undoubtedly naughty in the female's ear. Her heart slammed in her chest as she watched the flirty couple. She knew the Bruin well. Recognized him even before his scent drifted her way.

Crush Martinez.

Marty to his friends, but not to her. Betty and Crush were not friends. Hell, they were barely coworkers. Sure, she knew him as long as she'd known everyone else at the wedding. But working at Lance's Auto Repair for the last thirteen years together hadn't brought them any closer.

"Um, later Mel," she murmured, ignoring the laughter and smacking sounds of kisses as she walked hurriedly to her car.

Looked like a someone, make that a few someones, were getting lucky tonight, she mused tiredly.

Sad chuff.

"I know, girl," she told her inner Bear. "Someday we will meet our mate, but until then, it's home to Juniper and Cheeto. We'll water those babies, and snuggle in bed for some Firefly," she told herself.

Betty hummed along with the radio as she drove the short distance home, making it in a record thirteen minutes. She was tired, a little sad, and a little lonely. But her house plants and a little Mal Reynolds were bound to cheer her up.

It was the perfect end to an imperfect night. She strode from the car to her small rental house, careful of the wiggly brick walkway. As she neared the door, Betty turned her eyes upward and wished on the first star she saw.

"I'm not looking for miracles. I don't expect a big sexy Alpha to come rescue me or sweep me off my size nines. But a friend would be nice. Someone to snuggle up to and share a meal. I'm not asking for a mate. Just a friend," she said aloud, feeling foolish almost immediately.

Some folks thought wishing on stars was foolish, especially if the wisher believed in all that hocus pocus, but stranger things had happened in Barvale. Betty went inside and closed the door, shaking her head.

She did not notice the extra bright twinkling of the stars above her cozy little house. The constellation representing a certain trio of sisters watching from the heavens as one of their own called out for a friend.

When she went to sleep that night, she could have sworn she heard a velvety soft whisper in her ear as her head hit the pillow and her heavy eyes closed.

Sweet child, wishes do come true sometimes. You just have to believe.

Wouldn't that be nice? Betty thought as she sighed and slipped off into dreamland.

READ MORE WHEN YOU GRAB THE BOOK: www.cdgorri.com/books/bearly-friends

About the Author

C.D. Gorri is a USA Today Bestselling author of steamy paranormal romance and urban fantasy. She is the creator of the Grazi Kelly Universe.

Join her mailing list here: https://www.cdgorri.com/newsletter

An avid reader with a profound love for books and literature, when she is not writing or taking care of her family, she can usually be found with a book or tablet in hand. C.D. lives in her home state of New Jersey where many of her characters or stories are based. Her tales are fast paced yet detailed with satisfying conclusions.

If you enjoy powerful heroines and loyal heroes who face relatable problems in supernatural settings, journey into the Grazi Kelly Universe today. You will find sassy, curvy heroines and sexy, love-driven heroes who find their HEAs between the pages. Werewolves, Bears, Dragons, Tigers, Witches, Romani, Lynxes, Foxes, Thunderbirds, Vampires, and many more Shifters and supernatural creatures dwell within her worlds. The most important thing is every mate in this universe is fated, loyal, and true lovers always get their happily ever afters.

Want to know how it all began? Enter the Grazi Kelly Universe with Wolf Moon: A Grazi Kelly Novel or pick up Charley's Christmas Wolf and dive into the Macconwood Pack Novel Series today.

For a complete list of C.D. Gorri's books visit her website here:

https://www.cdgorri.com/complete-book-list/

Thank you and happy reading!

del mare alla stella,
    C.D. Gorri

Follow C.D. Gorri here:
    http://www.cdgorri.com
    https://www.facebook.com/Cdgorribooks

https://www.bookbub.com/authors/c-d-gorri

https://twitter.com/cgor22

https://instagram.com/cdgorri/

https://www.goodreads.com/cdgorri

https://www.tiktok.com/@cdgorriauthor